CALIBAN

BY LORINA STEPHENS

FIVE RIVERS PUBLISHING

WWW.FIVERIVERSPUBLISHING.COM

Five Rivers Publishing, 704 Queen Street, P.O. Box 293, Neustadt, ON N0G 2M0, Canada.

www.fiveriverspublishing.com

Edited by Dr. Robert Runté and Susan MacGregor.

Interior design and layout by Éric Desmarais.

Titles set in Caliban designed by John Benson. The font is named after Shakespeare's beast slave in The Tempest, Caliban represents Benson's attempt to tame crudely written letters into service.

Text set in PT Serif is a font family developed for the project "Public Types of the Russian Federation" dedicated to the 300 year anniversary of the civil type invented by Peter the Great.

Published in Canada

Library and Archives Canada Cataloguing in Publication

Stephens, Lorina J., author Caliban / by Lorina Stephens.

Issued in print and electronic formats.

ISBN 978-1-988274-34-8 (softcover)

I. Title.

PS8587.T4654C35 2017 C813'.54 C2017-904815-5

For Adam and Sara
and as always, for Gary

Contents

There can be an inherent bias in anthropological study. Perspective is everything.
REPORT FROM THE COMMISSIONER ON DREAMWEAVERS.

THE PROBLEM with what Jabod McCullough asked was it didn't make any sense. Why choose a permanent assignment Active on a quarantined planet? Tine asked that question.

"Because I think you're incorruptible," Jabod answered, his holo standing in one of the rocks Tine had been moving before the ping from his superior.

What was that supposed to mean? So Tine asked Jabod that.

"Let me answer by asking you a question: what are your aspirations?"

Aspirations? What was that? So Tine asked a third question.

"What would you like to see happen tomorrow, to you, to your brood, to your people?"

This was really going nowhere. *Incorruptible. Aspirations. Tomorrow.* Tine understood what those terms meant, but they had no relevance. Not for him. Not for any Caliban.

Instead of answering, he bent and put his shoulder to the rock he'd been moving to rebuild a floodwater diversion and shoved, digging his hooves into what purchase he could find on the hard-packed earth.

The rock gave, rolled, wobbled into the depression he'd made for it. Satisfied, he hunkered down to his haunches, looking out over the sere landscape—rock, dirt, desiccated shrubs of ochre, madder, sienna—and tried very hard to embrace those concepts Jabod put forward. Finally: "I would like enough food for my brood, to keep them safe from predators, to watch them learn enough so they can survive."

"And nothing else?"

He thought about that, about the things he'd been exposed to because of his privilege as an Active for the Interplanetary Criminal Investigations Bureau. All that information. All those holos of cultures and species, customs and regulations, an overwhelming glut of strange and stimulating experiences out there, so different from this planet he called home here on Setebos. Most of all, there were those artists known as dreamweavers, people able to manipulate reality and create living stories. That concept challenged everything he knew.

He looked up to Jabod's holo. "I would like to know more about dreamweavers."

"Why?"

"Because they manipulate the senses and can make you believe what they create is real."

"And that would benefit you how?"

"Were we to learn that skill, we would be better hunters and better able to ensure the life of the brood."

"So, your purpose is to protect the brood?"

"There is another purpose?"

Jabod took a few steps and his holo ended up

standing again in the rock Tine had just shoved into place. He wondered if Jabod was doing this on purpose, or if Tine's environment wasn't registering in Jabod's sensory display. It seemed ridiculous to be talking to a moving image of a human some light years away, and that thought brought him to the concept of time displacement, and once again to wrestle with what was real and what wasn't.

He rubbed the oil exuding from his warts into his belly, feeling his leathery hide beneath his fingers, aware of the aridity of the air, the glare of the sun. In the distance, he could hear his brood: laughter, the rumble of a warning growl, the skitter of beetles across red clay. He struck out and snatched one of the copper creatures and crunched down. Such a satisfying sound, even if this one wasn't particularly juicy.

"But I don't understand why you think you need me for this assignment," Tine said, shoving a wriggling antennae past his lips.

"Because you are the unexpected. Who would suspect you were working on an assignment for the Interplanetary Bureau of Investigations?"

Tine thought about that. There was plausibility to Jabod's reasoning, but there also wasn't. Any decent hunter knew it was better to sustain the illusion of normality to be successful, so why send in Tine? Further, how was Tine to make any kind of judgement about the success of this hunt—assignment, he supposed, was the correct term—if he didn't know anything about his prey or his prey's environment? For that matter, he didn't even know what this assignment was really about. He said that. Jabod demurred. Tine growled.

"I can't say anything more. I'm sorry, Tine. Not until we have you aboard an IPCIB ship where we know things are secure."

Oil now exuded freely from Tine's warts, rising with his own unease. He gave up massaging it into his hide. Jabod's statement was rife with subterfuge. How could Setebos not be secure? No one could land on this planet without risking spore invasion, perhaps die because of it. So how was an IPCIB liner more secure than here? He extended his claws and studied the gold fluidic circuitry on them that allowed him connection to the outside world. "You're sure spore withdrawal has been made safe?"

Tine watched Jabod's body language carefully now, for signs any hunter of skill would note. There were subtle signals. A wariness. Was it anxiety over whether Tine would accept the assignment, and risk his life in spore withdrawal? Was it something else?

The problem was, there wasn't enough information, and the only way Tine could obtain that information was to accept the assignment. He felt sure he was being manipulated. Maybe Jabod was also a skilled hunter. Even so, there was the lure of the dreamweavers, to meet one, perhaps many, perhaps even the Master dreamweaver herself, Ela. Wouldn't that be worth it? Wouldn't the knowledge he could gain from her benefit him and his brood?

Jabod took a few steps, his holo now sitting on the rock he'd been standing inside. The significance of that wasn't lost on Tine.

Finally, Tine said, "I accept."

He realized it came out in a bark, and that in itself was significant.

Jabod smiled and disappeared.

Tine snatched another beetle and crunched down. Every hunter knew you had to take risks. Surviving was hazardous. He wondered if he'd be successful in this hunt.

He stood and again set about shoving rocks back into a flood diversion. The rains would start any day now.

"YOU CAN'T run from what you are, Tine," Aganth said, all accusation gone from her voice.

He knew very well what he was. And that was the problem, wasn't it? He knew what he was. He always knew. He wanted to shout: *I'm Caliban, Aganth, bound to Setebos. Just like you!* He glared at his mate, hot with resentment, desperate to make her understand.

He could enumerate the obvious just to be confrontational. He could say he was a four-foot creature with a leathery hide and pocket-like warts, hooves for feet, and claws at his fingertips. Tine saw himself in Aganth, studied the yellow ovals of her eyes, the dark vertical pupils. There was a time, he realized, he thought her eyes were like niello on gold. Poetic.

If he was venturing down the poetic, albeit dark,

he could also enumerate the not so obvious: the spores. Everything always came back to the spores. The isolation of the planet because of the spores. The isolation of all life here because of the spores. Infection. Disfigurement. Incompatibility with everything not born to accept spores.

Setebos was under a United Order of Planets quarantine. And IPCIB was the body that regulated that quarantine, and the bureau for which Tine worked, and part of his present problem.

He huffed in derision, turned away. Anything not to look at her, not to see her confusion and distress, not to see his accusation reflected back at him, which turned out to be futile because he again saw himself in the carbonate of the window of the partition wall. He wondered if she had thought of him the same way. Had she seen his ancestry, the lineage of effective hunters? Had the thought of him ripping the entrails out of a kill been titillating? Did she like the illustrious nature of his natal brood?

He glanced at her, back to the window. He knew very well what he was. Every time he saw himself the accusation of what he was stared back.

Tine simmered there, choosing to ignore his wife's statement. She could always be so damnably serene. Serenity was the farthest thing from his mind. He rubbed the glands under his arms and massaged the oil into his hide.

He let his gaze fall beyond his reflection and out to the landscape of Setebos. It was as ugly as he felt. Rain hissed in a grey wall of torment. It had done so for six months now, over seven hundred days of spring monsoon. The sandstone scrubland had bloomed, flushing from red to green. He moved, hearing his hooves thud against the packed earth of the floor, feeling the liquid nature of the air. A breeze touched his face where he stood in the open arch.

It seemed only yesterday he'd been approached by Jabod McCullough to undertake an assignment. When there'd been no further mention of it, Tine assumed the entire situation had been resolved. In a way, he'd been relieved, but he'd also been disappointed. There was a certain thrill knowing he might risk his life to undertake a wider role in IPCIB, that he might get to meet a dreamweaver during that mission. But when he'd been called into service, and accepted, he'd consumed the resulting glut of information he'd been required to read, and now he also wished he'd never had that meeting with Jabod. It became clear to him how afraid the UOoP was of his planet and his species. While it hadn't been stated openly, Calibans were considered monsters, the spore a lethal contamination that might spread throughout the system should any Caliban survive withdrawal and travel off-planet.

Which brought him back to the rain and the reason he was waiting here with Aganth and his brood who were fidgeting and quarrelsome. Today was to be an auspicious day, a day of festival, a day the dormant seeds of the wailing trees sprouted. He could hear his brood behind him, see where some of them crouched in the other open portals. A pair of his girls did a rough and tumble on the covered pathway. He growled. They stopped, looked up at him, broke apart and hunkered quietly, their faces turned to the open landscape and the rain.

Like the incessant susurration of the rain, the sound of voices hissed around him. So many voices. So many of his brood here, both his and Aganth's natal relations, all of which meant too many bodies in too close a space, as far as he was concerned, even though brood members from other clutches had chosen to mark the day closer to home. Still, there were more than enough today, come to share in the spectacle of Setebos and the luxury he afforded. He growled again, wanting to display his displeasure, wanting against his better judgement for them to know.

Finally, he said, "I'm not running, Aganth." *Liar!* "I can't refuse the assignment."

"You told me years ago, your position as an Active with IPCIB was only honorary. Only to enforce UOoP law here."

"Well it was. It is. It—"

"It's complicated."

"Yes."

It was her turn to snarl now, to let her displeasure show. "Interplanetary Criminal Investigations Bureau—as if they're ever needed on Setebos."

Which meant what? he wondered. That he was redundant, a fool for thinking there was any honour accorded him because of his position? Now Aganth had chosen to berate him in front of their brood Calibans; it was nothing short of maddening. But he had chosen this occasion to tell her that his position as an IPCIB agent had changed. He should have said something of the possibility long ago. Her retaliation, he supposed, was understandable. Still. How was he to save face now?

In the end, it didn't matter. He shuddered. He could feel the seeds splitting open. Apparently so could many of the brood; there were gasps and cries all around. Again, he thought this was an awesome display of plant growth, even frightening, even though he'd been part of this all his life.

He shuddered once more when shoots burst out of the ground. The plants screamed. Soon the air vibrated with the cries of wailing trees. Aganth started a low ululation that oscillated with the screaming plants, and grew into a crescendo of pain.

His mouth fell open, noise torn from his throat. No Caliban could help but cry with the birthing trees. It was all part of symbiosis. It was the mark of Setebos.

The trees now writhed with growth, branches like snakes undulating from trunks. Buds formed, bulged, blew into leaves, and enlarged into Caliban-sized plates. The plants spiralled upward, cupping ponds of rain in the curling leaves. Twice Tine's height the trees grew, passed their height, upward, until they dwarfed not only him, but the sprawling worm of his home where every member of his brood cried out in sympathy, their voices a symphony of anguish.

His throat felt raw. The wailing of the trees slid down the scale. Leaves withered and exploded like bombs on the muddy ground. Branches wrenched to a halt and then bent, twisting into burled limbs, like his own, he thought.

Tine stilled, sucking in air, letting pain seep out and away. Aganth's ululation trembled, and then silenced. He stared at the trees, thinking about the pain and the ugliness of his planet. And now it would become truly ugly, for out of the ground burst newly hatched lizards, as yet flightless, that would race for the trees and a perch where they would feed on the secondary canopy and then fruit the trees would eventually bear.

It also meant a feeding frenzy on a delicacy Calibans enjoyed this once in four years. The young of his brood were the first to burst out into the dissipating rain, and sink long canines into soft bellies and tear, and laugh, and gulp down warm, tender flesh. He watched as adults followed, wallowing in mud, offering each other a choice leg, a munchable wing, a delicate head.

He remained where he was, fighting the desire to partake of this feast and feel the cool mud on his skin, the warm blood on his face. He thought again of what Aganth had said: *You cannot run from what you are.*

He wanted to say to her that by leaving the planet he could rid himself of the spore. All those holos had informed him he was ugly; his species was ugly. You could only spend so long staring at a kaleidoscope of cultures before you realized what you were part of was outside and beyond the weird and wide world of the UOoP. Sure, there were sentient and intelligent species of every elemental base imaginable out there, but there was nothing quite like a Caliban, a fact backed by news feeds which periodically reported on this quarantined planet, a planet subliminally feared by the remainder of the UOoP. The spore underscored that fear.

He turned, startled by Aganth's warmth by his side.

     CALIBAN

He watched the way she studied him, watched her fight her own desire to join their brood in the festival.

He told her what he'd just thought.

"And so you'd deny what all of us receive through our mothers' milk."

"You make the spore sound like a gift."

"Isn't it?"

He looked at her face, down the length of her brown, lumpy body, what he'd come to think of as deformity. "It leaves us ruined."

"It leaves us connected to our environments."

But there were all those images with which he'd gorged his imagination, humanoids with smooth skin, crowns of hair. Clothes. He wanted to be part of that, to be free of environmental sympathy, of ugliness. He was even willing to forfeit association with other Calibans to free himself of affliction. He would do anything not to feel the compulsion to be part of what he saw before him, what he had lived all his life doing, being.

Running was exactly what he had in mind.

"It's an assignment I must accept," he said after awhile, staring at the enormous trees.

"Your contract doesn't stipulate you must accept an assignment. Jabod knew the dangers when he enlisted you as the Caliban Active. Please, Tine, don't go. You need Setebos."

Tine thought about IPCIB. It was a glorified name for a policing unit organized to keep some form of order in his solar system. Twelve planets and forty man-made and natural satellites around two suns, a dense population, all under IPCIB's control.

All densely populated, that is, but Setebos.

You had to be born on Setebos to live there. Without the spore, Setebos meant death. The planet made no compromises. If you left, you never returned, or at least that was the prevailing theory. The spore in the pituitary died after twenty-four hours, although there was no hard evidence. Who would want to test that on a Caliban? Fine on sub-species. But unthinkable on a Caliban.

"Neither does my contract say I have the privilege to refuse," he answered. *I need you, Tine.* Jabod had said. *I need the skills of a Caliban on this assignment.* "They need an unlikely candidate to investigate Edain. I'm as unlikely as it gets."

"Edain's dangerous."

"What could be more dangerous than living the way we do? We're born racing to age. Before we know two days outside the womb we're physically adults, and we spend the rest of our lives becoming... becoming...." He turned away in disgust.

"Becoming something weathered by the elements," Aganth finished, her brown, leathery face wrinkling with concern. "There is no other planet which allows its inhabitants the freedom to find such beauty in so many ways."

"Beauty?" He glared at her. "Look at yourself, Aganth! You're ugly! Ugly couldn't look any worse!" He watched his cruelty take its toll, watched her exercise control.

You're a real prince of a prick, he thought, knowing full well Aganth deserved none of his hostility and all his regard. But she didn't understand, couldn't understand the lure of life free from this entangled, demanding symbiosis was a hope greater than the sum of his paltry existence. There was so much to know. There was so much to experience. Four months and so much had changed.

"I'm considered very beautiful," she said at length. He heard the hurt in her voice, the bewilderment with his unnatural attraction to things ersatz. "That's why you took me for your mate—because I'm beautiful. You had to surround yourself with everything of beauty. Is that why you'll go to Edain? To find out about beauty?"

"No! It's strictly business!"

Her purple, lipless mouth twisted. "And you have no curiosity about people who sculpt mountains by thinking? About painters who use light? About dreamweavers? None of these titillate you?"

"I've told you already—this is strictly business. They've had a murder there for the first time in their history." He looked down and away from her, feeling a traitor, feeling a coward.

"A history of fifteen years."

Commissioner Jabod McCullough hadn't seemed surprised about the Gelt Ambassador's disappearance and now assumed death. Tine couldn't resist questioning Jabod about that. And Tine's instincts had proven right: Jabod had felt uneasy about letting the Gelt go alone to meet the Edain Guild. There had been more to Jabod's concern, but Tine had been unable to discover what. Tine was sure there was something unusual about the Gelt's disappearance. Hard proof was what was needed here.

"They've been peaceful until now," he said.

"I should think that would be a warning to you."

"About what?"

"About the dangers of superficial beauty."

His gaze shot back up at her, violence an imperative in his fingers. "You're being ridiculous."

"And what about the risks of spore withdrawal?"

"Jabod says they think they've perfected a treatment."

"And you're volunteering to test that?"

"Yes."

"You'd risk death for this assignment?"

"Yes."

"You must truly hate us all and yourself."

How was he supposed to answer that?

"We'll see, Tine." She turned her back to leave and join the others. "You'll have to divorce me before going tomorrow. All your rights, per Caliban law, will be revoked."

How could she do this to him? Ah, but she wasn't serious. Surely this was Aganth's way of issuing an ultimatum. He was, after all, the sire of this brood of eighteen. He and Aganth's fecundity was part of their wealth. They moved only in the best of Caliban circles. "You're not going to invoke those antiquated laws!"

"I am."

He felt the shock of that, watched her for any telltale signs of distress, for oils exuding from her skin, for that scent like wet rope. But no. Her skin remained dry. None of her warts opened and closed like miniature mouths. No purple flushed her flesh.

She was serious!

She glanced back at him, her face inscrutable. "You'll be no good to us here on Setebos. By killing the spore, you will have killed our allegiance. Our brood will renounce you as their father. You're free, Tine. Go and make your discoveries."

He watched her leave, heard her hooves on the pounded earth of the floor, heard the festival beyond, and voices raised in question.

Any colonist will attempt to name and normalize surroundings, even if that means transplanting the old into the new. It's not only a trait as ancient as history, but a trait which we now know to be destructive: familiar surroundings breed familiar sociological problems.

IPCIB Operations Manual

THE AIRLOCK hissed closed when Tine stepped into the isolation chamber. Out the windows he could clearly see the Caliban landscape—a dun and rose-coloured terrain made warm from the glow of the second rising sun. The first was setting to the north. Sulphurous puddles glinted like ancient treasures in the golden light. The trees that sprouted yesterday now cupped the yellow sky, and around them, in a carpet of pastel, bloomed ground creepers fed from the nutrients in the falling leaves. Were he outside, he knew he'd hear the chittering of the newly-born and surviving lizards. On cue, one of the iridescent reptiles flew from one branch to another.

Tine lifted his gaze to the distant terraces where striated rocks flowed like waterfalls and faded into mauve and azure blurs. Daily the landscape would unfold in a series of plant rebirths. That ephemeral process sometimes continued for three years, and then subsided into the year of austerity. The ground would bake to a pale grey then, and people like Aganth would rake the ground at their feet into patterns.

Today would have been the day he'd have sung the ritual of gathering, a time when the first, sweet plant-stuffs would be harvested against the year of austerity, while the hunters of the brood would return in shifts with small game to be processed and dried. Aganth would have sung with him, his brood filling his home with harmony. There would have been laughter. Aganth would make him laugh. She had always been adept at that. Even that first courting took place on a day like today, Aganth laughing that gentle, sharing laugh when he'd let his warts open and close in prenuptial overtures.

Don't think! Don't remember!

A hot lump sat in his belly, threatening to consume him with grief.

A divorce! He hadn't thought that far, hadn't even considered his union would be redundant, ridiculous if he were leaving. He wouldn't be back. Couldn't. What was he doing?

Alone. A solitary Caliban. What was that? All his years cancelled through the vehicle of fifteen moments of Caliban ritual. At first dawn, he'd walked through the arch of his family's arms, knowing as he passed, each of them broke the arch, giving him their backs. The pyre of his sparse belongings even now filled his memory with heat, consuming, compassionless, a cold kind of killing heat.

He was divorced, homeless, a pariah in the way of Caliban things.

He lingered a little longer over the view, unwilling

to embark on this journey with such sorrow, such bereavement as his farewell. Such portent. No one would come to see him on his way. It wasn't good to go in search of new things with such ill will on his heels. He jerked his head, turned his back to Setebos and stepped toward the remote clinic IPCIB had landed just beyond his garden, linked by a sterile tunnel to this isolation chamber. As he approached, a voice said, "Palm to the palmlock, please."

He glanced around, a growl in his throat.

"Palm to the palmlock, please."

He looked at the wall in front of him, a shatterproof bio-composite glass. There were two panels set to left and right—he assumed the palmlocks the voice had indicated. He raised his left hand, pressed his palm as flatly to the panel as possible without unsheathing his claws. There was a hiss and then an entry that hadn't been there a moment before melted open.

He growled again, feeling unhinged, unsure, realizing he was ill-prepared for this adventure. If he was incapable of processing this, how would he be on Edain?

"Step into the chamber, please."

Again, he looked around himself, wondering where the imaging centre was located, and realized the system was probably imbedded in the bio-comp. He stepped into the tiny cubicle. The wall flowed back into place. This time he didn't growl.

The isolation chamber was sterile by comparison to the landscape. A glaring, blue-white light filled the cramped cubicle. A cot was against one wall. The other two walls were a grotesque assortment of floating digital data about which he could only speculate, and which hadn't been apparent from the outside.

"Lay down on the cot," the disembodied voice said. The voice sounded bored.

He stood there, disoriented, staring at the white cot. Part of him longed to thrash against the walls and claim Setebos; another part of him was eager to continue with this mission. There were new things to discover, new vistas to carve. And he wanted to be exhilarated by all that newness. That other part of him wanted no part of newness. He thought of dreamweavers then—the artists who wove stories so real you lived them. Their legend was all the lure he needed.

"Lay down on the cot," the voice repeated. "Lay down on the cot."

Tine flinched. His gaze darted to the sterile-looking cot. He couldn't imagine a bed like that being used for anything but sterile functions. An image of the bed he'd shared with Aganth erupted. He felt like he'd explode with memory.

It was all he could do to control his reactions, to conceal what he felt. There were aliens watching, aliens unfamiliar with the way of Setebos, of Calibans.

Don't turn back, he thought. *They'll think you're just one of those creatures of a backwater planet.*

He lay on the hard, composite palette. The data in the air exploded with information. He sat up. The data died.

"Lay down on the cot," the voice insisted. "The

bio-table will monitor your progress during spore withdrawal."

He returned to a recline, watchful, distrustful of his environment.

Spore withdrawal.... Progress during spore withdrawal.

There was something very final in that statement. He wondered if it wouldn't mean his own death. Spore withdrawal, he'd heard, wasn't an easy process: disorientation, tunnel vision, acute auditory perceptions, fevers, convulsions. If you advanced as far as convulsions it usually meant death. He'd seen the bodies of those who attempted to leave Setebos. It had been horrifying, even for someone accustomed to the planet's harshness. That had been twenty years ago, when Setebos first allied with the UOoP. Since then, physical associations with the outside world had been non-existent. The rest of the solar system knew about Setebos through feeds and holos. It was too dangerous to visit. It was too dangerous to leave.

How badly do I need to leave? Had Aganth been right?

The cot warmed. Brilliance burst around him. Before he could react, light flashed across his body, prickling and intense. His felt his mouth gaping.

The voice said, "Your surface epidermis has been destroyed to inhibit spore invasion. The chamber is completely sterile."

He closed his mouth. Part of the table wrapped up over his mouth, injected something bitter before he could react and then retracted. Another part dropped moisture into his eyes. Something invaded his rectum. It felt as though ice were running through his system.

"Is this really necessary?" he said, panting from the invasion.

"It's necessary," the voice answered. "Relax. We don't get our giggles doing this stuff. We're injecting you with octobots."

He squirmed but accepted the situation. The probes retreated, their payload apparently delivered. He felt his muscles relax. The light shifted to ultra-violet.

"To protect you from jaundice," the voice said before Tine could form a question.

"I suppose you can read my mind now."

"Something like that. Enjoy the next twenty-four hours. Sing out if you feel like someone to talk to."

Tine only nodded. Sing out? He wondered if he should start humming a tune. Was there ritual with these people also? Was there something he should do?

For awhile he lay there, waiting for some instruction, staring at the surroundings which had dulled to white, all data gone. There was nothing on which to focus. Nowhere he could distract himself.

He wondered if those thousands of octobots were now in his brain, delivering his thoughts in data dumps: cranial chemical analysis, chest for cardiac, body temperature. Spiked for sound. *If I fart will I send their feed off the chart?*

"You just might," said that voice.

He grinned broadly.

His grin faded. He thought about how much of his body they could control with those octobots, and just how accustomed he was to having autonomy of his life. He was losing some of that autonomy with the death of the spore. Now there would be no excuse to refuse IPCIB demands. It had been convenient to be an agent on permanent assignment. Jabod had known that to place Tine outside Setebos would have been an unwarranted risk, and only now Tine appreciated the commissioner's concern.

"It's important you relax."

Could they hear him? What if they didn't have the right clearance?

"We do."

So, they could hear him. He growled, wishing he could tear open his flesh and purge his system of this infinitesimally small invasion.

"We need to adjust the flow," he heard them say. "This isn't standard."

Well of course this wasn't standard. When had they ever successfully purged a Caliban of Setebos?

"Those levels are better."

After several hours chewing the situation, Tine lost recognition of his surroundings. Detachment multiplied his growing alarm. He couldn't remember consenting to this violation. Panic pushed his gaze around the room. He felt as though he were at the bottom of a purple well. The octobots, he was sure, were dancing across his chest, forming patterns and loops. He could hear the chatter of information and the booming of his own heart-lung.

"He's hallucinating."

"I've got it."

One part of his body told him this was part of

spore withdrawal. That part was clinical, like an automaton programmed for service. Instinct formed the opposing part of his body, and he now railed at himself to tumble from the table and float free.

His muscles spasmed. For a moment, he wondered if there had been a tremor. He discounted that thought; the isolation chamber was cushioned with one of the best shock absorbers. Distantly, he speculated if he might be fevered.

Those disembodied voices confirmed that.

After several hours, Tine was sure his bones screamed. He thrashed in a fluid bath, yanking against his invisible harness. Memory of being placed in the oily fluid evaded him, and that sent his fears slamming through him. That the bath was to lower his body temperature might have been a possibility. What was a certainty was pain, fear, and anger.

They'd restrained him!

This, also, passed.

"We're removing you to a place of rest," a distant voice said.

The consonants clashed against his ears, the softer sounds sibilant. He looked everywhere, frightened, exhausted, feeling like brown jelly as grav-lifts shifted him from the bath to the cot.

"We done?" he managed to ask.

"We're done."

"And I'm alive."

"Alive and spore-free."

Exhaustion won out and left him giddy. He'd survived spore withdrawal. Crowned in triumph,

Tine ignored the fact he was peeing prodigiously, everywhere in fact.

"When do we leave?" he managed to ask.

"As soon as we remove you to medical. Tell me something—why would you want to leave Setebos? It's incredible."

Tine's triumph died.

Perhaps Setebos never leaves, he thought.

We don't fully understand yet how dreamweavers incarnate characters, or even why. What they have told us is they create their own realities. Some of them even believe other dreamweavers are products of their own creation. What we have physically been able to prove is dreamweavers are somehow capable of creating matter, and we have proven that fact through reversal; that is, the matter they create has shown no place or point of origin in any of our tests. It is, however, difficult for us to believe our tests, because there is every indication we're dealing with something which is perhaps, quite literally, universal in scope. Dreamweavers themselves have admitted to creating our realities. What we must now attempt to prove is the difference between reality and illusion, in a game with no rules. It is a laughable problem: science is nothing but rules.

REPORT FROM THE COMMISSIONER ON DREAMWEAVERS.

JABOD MCCULLOUGH stood listening to the murmur of business on the bridge of an IPCIB ship, aware of the deference he was being offered, the buffer of space the captain and crew made for him.

He heard the captain ask: "You have an approach vector?"

"Affirmative, Captain," the navigator responded, and then rattled off coordinates.

"Carry on."

Jabod watched as officers poked and swiped at floating information, turned his attention to the central display where the ball representing Setebos hung, the glowing spike of the transportation run tethering the docking station.

It had been twelve years, he realized, he'd been doing this, shouldering what it meant to be the Commissioner of the Interplanetary Criminal Investigations Bureau.

"We will be initiating all security protocols," the captain said to him.

"Before we dock, I'm assuming."

"Yes."

"Good."

Damn right, after that shit-show around the Gelt Ambassador. Missing? How the hell had that happened? On his watch!

He thought he'd seen just about everything a criminal could do, from spectacular embezzlement schemes and political sabotage, to full out hack-and-scatter serial murders and pirate-slavers. It was because of that experience he had personally escorted the Gelt Ambassador to Edain. An envoy from the asteroid belt of mines needed high protection. Where there was wealth, there was also threat of assassination or kidnapping and ransom, or all three combined, and Jabod had wanted to be sure his charge arrived safely, because it wouldn't do to piss off the Gelt Consortium. The entire solar system's mineral supply was in the Consortium's hands, and the Gelts were a tetchy lot, sensitive to perceived slight, preferring miscommunication to communication, sometimes to the point it seemed they just plain delighted in shoveling shit against rapidly rotating blades.

And now the Ambassador was missing, presumed dead.

"There's a call for the Commissioner," the communications officer said.

Jabod shot her a look. "Who?"

"The Vice-chair of the Gelt Consortium."

"I'm unavailable."

"They are quite insistent, Commissioner."

"I'm sure they are. Tell them I'm in a meeting with the Edain Guild."

"They're calling for charges and a trial. They're talking about a death sentence."

Jabod paused a moment, wondering if that idiot Vice-chair had simply blurted everything he was thinking to this poor communications officer. Kill the messenger. Hell, why not kill the messenger if you can't reach the alleged criminal?

"Tell the Vice-chair I apologize for the inconvenience and that I cannot speak directly with him now, but I will be pleased to have a conversation with him later today. If he protests further, simply put him into a queue."

The officer nodded, and sub-vocalized that information.

A fatwa? As if this eye for that tooth would conjure the Ambassador back into existence.

He turned to his aide who did his best to be invisible at his shoulder. "Implement the media campaign."

"Done."

Jabod watched as the aide conducted an information symphony without aid of a baton. With that action, he now had every available arm of IPCIB feeding garbage information to media, doing everything to misguide, miscommunicate, misinterpret anything and everything leaking out of his information dam. There had been special dispatches and aides to Gelt, multi-species Actives as distantly related to Jabod's human ancestry as possible in the hope any accusations of human-supremacy conspiracies could be smothered. At the risk of stating the obvious it was a political and media carnival, and Jabod intended to be the master of this ring, not some by-blow act. Things were so tense he'd even resorted to the considerable influence and talent of Ela, the Master Dreamweaver on Edain, the very head of the Edain Guild. Damn it all, it might not be enough, and that was why he'd finally succumbed to Ela's suggestion that he pull in Tine. She'd observed that a Caliban, with not only the instincts of his kind, but the training of an IPCIB active, would be the perfect candidate to investigate the disappearance of the Gelt Ambassador, and moreover, could keep the investigation discreet. Jabod had demurred, he remembered, arguing the dangers of spore withdrawal.

He remembered clearly the way she'd smiled. "You know he'll survive."

Indeed, he did know Tine would survive. But he wondered how it was she could know that. In the end, he dismissed her statement as confidence in Tine's ability to survive, rather than knowledge of why IPCIB had kept Setebos in isolation all these years.

"We'll be docking in three minomes, Commissioner," said the captain.

Three minomes, three minutes—time meant what you wanted.

Jabod's attention swung away from the captain to the display. It occurred to him, as he watched the white light of the run draw closer, the only planet in the two solar systems without the Guild's influence was Setebos. Jabod wondered just what that would mean now, both for Setebos and the rest of the United Order of Planets.

He thought of Tine waiting at the other end of the run. What would Tine think of Guild representation on that austere, oppressive planet known as Setebos? Undoubtedly, the Caliban would say something derisive. Art on a backwater planet, Tine would ask? Impossible. Setebos would deny advancement. And Jabod knew it was Setebos the physical entity, not Setebos the political that would create that denial. The planet was in isolation because of a spore that claimed the pituitary as its host. Setebos, despite sophisticated link communication, was as isolated as a planet in plague.

At this moment, Jabod wished he had one of Tine's cryptic comments. The Caliban would be sure to make sense of his foreboding. The last time Jabod hovered on the end of a transport run the Gelt Ambassador had gone missing. Nothing apparently had been wrong with the run. As far as the techs were concerned the Ambassador had arrived on Edain. Ela had assured IPCIB the Ambassador most assuredly had not arrived, and every member of the Guild in attendance that day had corroborated her statement.

Different run, Jabod told himself. Same ship. His ship. His people. They'd all checked out.

The Gelt Ambassador had been impatient, he remembered, fussing with the elaborate costume in which he'd rigged himself. There had been enough wealth woven into the gold material to keep Tine's brood for several months, assuming the Caliban might have to employ currency to survive. Jabod remembered wondering if it wasn't a little overkill on the part of the Ambassador, and if ultimately it wasn't a statement of Gelt culture, the flash and dazzle of a collective corporate mind that evaluated a thing, or person, by what return could be realized on the investment of something even so immaterial as a conversation.

And yet here, in this same spot, Tine would appear, without any display of wealth, with his only currency the efficacy of his wit and reason. The thought of investment wouldn't occur to Tine. Jabod was only too aware Tine's focus was in the now. Conditioned by environment, governed by spore and species and symbiosis; the past was something from which one gained experience, the future would be what it would be, and the only matter of import was what you did now, and then now, and then now again.

Protect us all, Jabod thought, if the Calibans ever figure out they can leave Setebos. Their approach to life could end up being a compelling philosophy that might sweep the UOoP, and that was something the brokers of influence and power wouldn't appreciate.

But, then, the Calibans must want to leave, and in that regard Tine was an exception.

"Docked, and link with run established, Captain," the navigator said.

"We're here, Commissioner," the captain said in turn.

"Of course," Jabod replied. And without waiting for a response, Jabod left the bridge. He realized he was the first person to ever meet a Caliban face to face, a distinction that wasn't lost on him given the Captain's hesitation. He paused at the porthole to the bridge, looked over his shoulder. "Captain?"

"I'll be along directly, Commissioner."

"Indeed." Jabod left and made his way to the run's docking platform. To his surprise, it was the Master Dreamweaver Ela who greeted him once there, and for a moment speculation and calculation ran through his head.

"You're wondering why and how I'm here," she said.

He noticed there was a faint radiance around her, for a moment thought her naked and then realized she wore a flesh-toned garment that clung to her like a second skin. Vaguely he wondered how she'd manage to pee in a getup like that. He then noticed there was no one else at the docking platform, and no one manning the transportation run. It was eerily quiet; just the faint hiss of the run in the background, an itch on the skin from its power. Its light filled the room.

He found himself in a defensive stance, instinct and training kicking in where apparently his ability to reason did not. It's just that there was no possible way Ela could be standing there, watching him with those enormous, wide eyes, that mouth set in an ambiguous smile. She was supposed to be on Edain, not here on this ship orbiting Setebos.

"Do you wonder why I'm here?"

"Understatement," he said at length.

"You're in no danger."

He glanced around. Where were the technicians and duty officer of this deck? How could he have overlooked this? "Where's the crew?"

She shrugged, an elegant and slight gesture. "They found there were other imperatives that took their attention."

"Then how—"

"Did I get here?" She took a step closer to him, fitted her arm under his and leaned close to his ear. He was overwhelmed with a sense of enormous import, of events expanding beyond his control. Had he ever had control, he wondered vaguely. *How the hell did she get on this ship?* "That's not the question you should be asking."

He shivered, fighting his sense of unreality, and thought to take her arm and twist it into a hold, but she slid out of the movement like water sliding around an obstacle.

"Where's Tine?" he demanded, glaring at her.

"Ah, now you're getting closer. He's ascending."

"But—"

"Ascent should be virtually instantaneous?"

"Yes."

"It is. There's nothing wrong with the run."

    Caliban

"Then—"

"Where is he? Coming, Commissioner. But for you to understand that, I'm afraid I have to show you something else, and that's going to require a subterfuge with which you're unwittingly going to assist. You're in no danger so long as you keep a firm grasp on reality, and allow yourself to accept there are possibilities in the universe none of you have ever conceived."

None of you have ever conceived. Why did that ring so discordantly? In the moment it took for him to analyze that thought, a new reality confronted him, one that looked, walked, talked like him. Was him. A mirror. A clone. He stood there looking at himself. Himself smiled.

"A thread, actually," it said.

None of you.

"A thread," he said, thinking out loud. It occurred to him he should be alarmed.

"A character a dreamweaver creates," she said.

He worked through that, then: "None of *us,*" and she nodded.

"Yes. None of you."

"You're different," he said.

"Yes."

"Different species."

"Yes." She took his hand now, gestured with the other to his clone which nodded and stood back. "I'm sorry it has to be this way, Commissioner, but it's imperative Tine makes certain discoveries on Edain, for your sake, for his sake, for sake of my own kind."

She pulled him into the light of the run, and he felt himself falling toward an unknown destination.

TRAVELLING ABOARD an IPCIB liner was equal to, if not better than, travelling aboard resort liners, Tine speculated, although certainly he had no real experience with either, and certainly the criteria he presently used was one tender to every Caliban's heart—food. No hunting, no gathering, no preparation required. Just tap in your choice on the table's menu board and as if spirited, there it arose through the table like some morphing miracle. And apparently if you didn't like the bill of fare you could simply pinch the menu between fingers, expand it in the air with your conductive polished claws—Tine's were gold because he liked the shine—and draw or describe in text what you wished. Of course, his claws were so covered in food now, he'd have to do a thorough grooming before they'd likely work with any degree of accuracy. He didn't care. The food was—what was that term Jabod used so often?—ah yes, fucking wonderful.

Even so, he wondered how IPCIB could afford these luxuries. He'd never had so much food at his disposal, how he wanted, when he wanted, which was often.

With Setebos it was feast or famine, and in times of feast, it was orgiastic. You ate till you puked and then you ate some more, because it was so good and so bountiful and who cared about the attendant pain, because there was food now, right now.

He shoved a strand of fowl past his teeth, at the same time spearing a mound of green flower buds which were steamed to a perfect balance between crunch and mush. Interesting, this concept of subjecting food to heat. In some cases, heat enhanced flavour. Seared meat, he decided, was spectacular. He flared his olfactory warts in dissatisfaction, however, at the steamed vegetables. Much better crunchy and crisp. Yes, that was thing he decided: keep your food crunchy and crisp. Nothing quite so satisfying as a good snap, crunch and pop. He did miss the hunt, the adrenaline flow, the satisfaction of stalking and successfully bringing down anything from mouthful to village-feeding prey, the feel of his fangs and claws sinking into a neck, the snap of a spine, the tearing of skin and tendons and drip of blood. But given it wouldn't do to hunt the crew, what was offered from food services was certainly acceptable.

He studied the tined thing in his fingers—tined—barked a laugh at the play on words, and wondered about this tool affectation, couldn't see the point or need or advantage using the apparatus. In fact, it could be downright painful if your aim was off, and navigating the thing past his canines was interesting. He glanced over to the tray beside him where there was an avalanche of dinnerware—another thing he found odd, their need to put food on and in things. He belched loudly to express his pleasure with his feast, grinned toothily at the glances from some of his fellow diners, and quaffed his third glass of that fermented fruit stuff. Quite good. Now if he could just get his head to stop feeling like it was floating on the ceiling.

By the time he devoured his fourth sweet course—a delicate, rolled ground grain of some sort, drizzled with a distilled orange concoction and the lactation of some beast—that at least he could identify—and filled with multi-coloured berries, another guest joined the mess—both the place and the condition. For a moment, Tine continued to savour the bouquet of tastes in his mouth, but when the newcomer remained beside his table, Tine turned his attention from his pleasure, letting out a low growl.

He swallowed, sputtering, "Excuse me, Commissioner! I had no idea—"

"I'm glad to see withdrawal hasn't diminished your appetite." Jabod McCullough smiled, gestured to Tine's discarded dishes. "And I'm glad we finally meet face to face."

It was likely he'd made a complete spectacle of himself. He glanced up at the other patrons who had given him a width berth—something to which he'd become accustomed—most of them human, tried to figure out their expressions, decided his supposition that he'd allowed himself to become a spectacle was correct. To rescue his dignity, he borrowed from research and dabbed at his mouth with the cloth thing they seemed to affect as part of polite society. He wasn't quite sure why it was necessary for people to press cloth to mouth, but he was certain doing so was an indication of culture. Only problem was, the cloth came away smeared with the detritus of his feast. He suspected a great deal of that feast remained on his face, which would be fine among his own people, but he'd learned from all the holos he'd studied for years that what was customary on Setebos was not elsewhere in the UOoP. A glance at his chest confirmed he'd simply been himself. He started to swipe at the smears, gave up when some of his warts oozed and he was left no choice but to massage that into his hide, aware humans didn't do anything of the sort. But it was that or let the amber fluid trickle down his skin, and it occurred to him touching himself might be a preferable alternative to oozing warts. Judging from the horrified looks from some of the crew, probably not.

He shoved his hands under the table. "I apologize, Commissioner."

Jabod smiled. Tine wondered what that meant. "Every chef should have a Caliban to feed."

Again, Tine sputtered apologies.

"Tine, really!" Jabod laughed. "I complimented you!"

He sobered. Why had he been complimented? "Yes, sir. Am I to be briefed?" Cosseted, instructed, indulged like an infant in civilization?

Tine was aware Jabod studied him. He tried to compose his features, to make his face less ugly, less ferocious and gave up. It wasn't as though he could, at will, rearrange his anatomy. And so what if the rest of the UOoP were horrified by his kind? Fuck all those holos he'd seen.

"I thought I'd brief you as soon as you were able,"

Jabod said. "My apologies we couldn't have finally met under more pleasant circumstances."

Tine nodded, waiting, assessing. Why did he have the feeling something wasn't right? He kept feeling like he was on the hunt, and as a result his warts kept oozing.

Jabod touched the *clear* tab on the table and the remnants of Tine's feast melted into the composite. It was then Tine realized they were alone, that all other patrons had discreetly exited when Jabod sat down.

Debriefing here? Why here? Why displace all the crew?

"You're aware how Edain, as a political entity, came to be?" Jabod asked.

So right to it. Tine watched as Jabod sat across the table from him.

He thought about what Jabod just asked, considered the implications of his answer, and the details pertinent to that. Setebos had only been in the UOoP for twenty years, and even then had been isolated from interplanetary association. The spore predetermined that, and was indiscriminate about who or what it invaded, adapting with what most of the UOoP considered viral efficiency. However, despite the quarantine, every Caliban knew Edain's story, knew how it was a conclave of utopians created a sanctuary where they could live in independent determination.

Tine responded, adding that Edain, a world rich with natural resources, was deeded to those in search of a paradise which nurtured and celebrated creation. "It's now the mecca of artistic study in our end of the universe," he said.

"And the Edains are with power," Jabod added. "They have a seat like everyone else in the UOoP Chamber."

"Perhaps it's a little subtler than that."

"Subtle?"

"Even Setebos has a seat on the UOoP Chamber, albeit we attend virtually. But we remain in isolation despite all we could offer to the UOoP.

"Edains, however, have a working ambassadorial envoy on every known world. Everyone's culture sifts through Edain hands. There isn't another member of the UOoP that has that privilege, has gained that trust."

"Everyone's culture sifts through their hands except Setebos."

Tine flinched. "Except Setebos."

"Exactly why you're here."

"I don't understand."

"You're uninvolved enough to be trusted."

So, it was a matter of trust. But why not trust the policing forces and governing body on Edain? And why bring in an investigator who would be, by no means, invisible? By UOoP standards he, like all Calibans, was functionally illiterate. Himself, he couldn't see the advantage in being able to read and write if all that information were available in holo-form. That handicap, and he was sure the literate world of the UOoP would regard Calibans as intellectually handicapped, would most definitely mark him and his kind, render him conspicuous if literacy were required on this mission. That brought him back to the question: if this entire situation required delicacy and subterfuge, why him? Why a Caliban? Why draw attention in this manner?

Tine realized he should have thought of this sooner, that he'd been blinded by the lure of adventure, the scent of the hunt. Perhaps he'd even been naïve, out of his depth. There was no questioning his prowess as a hunter on his home-world, but his instincts told him he was being played.

"So, what's happening on Edain?" he asked when Jabod remained silent, unabashedly studying him.

"Nothing confirmed."

Tine thought about that, then: "So, I'm under cover."

"An envoy from Setebos to negotiate the establishment of one of Edain's illustrious entourages."

Which statement also required thought, until: "While covertly investigating—"

"What appears to be a murder. But we're not sure murder has been committed."

"That was in the preliminary holo you sent me. Forgive me, Commissioner, but it sounds like you want me to chase ghosts."

"Something like that."

Tine growled. Jabod's attention flicked to Tine's fingers where he could feel his claws flexing, the gold conductive polish gleaming.

"Can you control that?" Jabod nodded to Tine's hands.

Tine wondered why Jabod should ask that, whether the question was born of fear of latent violence, or xenophobia, or merely curiosity. "When I want." He retracted his claws.

"When you're on Edain?"

Tine smiled. He knew it would appear like a snarl, and at that point didn't really care if he alarmed the Commissioner, because it was now apparent he was indeed being played. "If I'm threatened, no one will know until it's too late."

Jabod nodded, apparently accepting Tine's assertion. Tine knew the Commissioner had studied holos of him hunting. When their weekly virtual meetings wandered from business to personal, they'd periodically discussed his ability to keep a growing brood supplied with protein.

"The mission has to be covert," Jabod said. "We can't prove this alleged murder actually took place on Edain, or for that matter if we're dealing with a kidnapping. As you may know, the planet purports a crimeless society."

Which brought Tine to consider the inferences around Jabod's statement; that word *purports*. It was as though Jabod found the concept of a society without crime something beyond credibility, and that in turn said a great deal about both this man to whom he was now answerable, and the UOoP as a whole. Finally, he said, "But you suspect."

"Yes."

"Why?"

"Logically speaking, what other reason could there be? The Gelts haven't exactly made friends in the UOoP. There are a lot of culture clashes happening because of them, all stemming from economic disparities." He shrugged. "The whole mining consortium of Gelt could blow up in our faces if we don't figure this out quickly. They're already asking why the Ambassador's liner has been delayed, and unhappy their negotiations to obtain mining rights for Edain's natural resources have been stalled. Keeping this covered isn't easy."

That required some thought. "So, this hasn't been released for public knowledge?"

Jabod shook his head.

"Why would the Edains kill the Gelt Ambassador? There's nothing to be gained."

"Superficially. But we suspect more. Over six years we've compiled a file on every dignitary, potentate, government official and military head who has visited Edain. The resulting theories are startling, albeit speculative."

"Sounds like you were investigating a murder before it even occurred."

"We had reason to suspect something like this might happen. One of my valuable Actives went to Edain. After she returned she seemed...." He shrugged. "Different. We ran checks on her personality profile. At first, we found nothing. But one of our operatives dug a little deeper and found slight differences in emotional triggers, variations in memory recall—"

"You mine data on us?"

Jabod smiled apologetically. "I can't have sabotage within IPCIB. It's necessary."

So how much of his own life did they monitor? "How long did it take to compile this data? Sounds painstaking."

"It was. And is."

"And that means you're going to continue to have me monitored?" He'd put it out there now, the bait, the notice that he knew he was little more than a counter in IPCIB's game.

"That translator with which you've been implanted is also a monitor, yes. I'm sorry. Nothing is sacrosanct, Tine. Not here. Not now. Failing to take these measures would be sloppy, especially in an organization like ours. You know that."

So, they *had* been spying on him. "Continue," said Tine, wondering for how long he'd been monitored on Setebos, and how they'd managed to do that. He'd always wondered why it was so necessary to the UOoP to have an IPCIB Active on his planet. It wasn't like anyone could just come and go at leisure. So why have surveillance on a quarantined planet that had no technology for off-planet travel?

Finally, Jabod said: "It was ascertained my Active on Edain had been replaced, either by a clone, or something else."

"Such as?"

"I'll get to that."

Evasion again.

"We monitored Edain's visitors," Jabod said. "We found that some very important people were illustrating my Active's symptoms."

"Such as?"

"Such as government officials, heads of corporations, religious leaders—"

"You think there's some kind of plot?" Which seemed ridiculous, the stuff of fiction.

"Something like that. But, again, we're not sure. There's no reason for Edains to overthrow existing governments. They already have a monopoly on the arts."

And while Tine knew he was utterly unprepared for this wide, weird world, he also realized his native instincts might just serve him well. "You've overlooked something." And that was how a hunter tracked prey, by never overlooking the minutia.

"Oh?"

"When economies spiral down instead of up, one of the first areas to suffer is the arts. The UOoP has been in a slump for a decade." At least the other planets of the UOoP had been in a slump. Little affected Setebos. Tine knew all this from endless observation. And it now occurred to him maybe there were benefits in their isolation.

Jabod grinned. "Of course! If Edains could replace government, military and religious heads with their own people, they could perform a mass ideological change which would ensure the proliferation of the arts."

"Not a bad idea, if done properly."

Jabod's brow arched.

"Just an observation, Commissioner." He kept his gaze fixed upon Jabod's face. "What's the something else with which these potentates could be replaced?"

"You've seen a dreamweaver performance?"

"I've seen a streamed holo."

"Then you know a weaver incarnates a story so it's presented somewhat in the way of a play. You have heard of a play?"

Just how much of an idiot did he think Tine was? As if Calibans had no culture of their own, as if oral traditions weren't one of the foundations of their heritage. Tine didn't even bother to respond and gestured for Jabod to get on with it.

"The weavers who populate the planets outside Edain are at the low end, sort of a division of recruiting officers for the Edain Guild. They can sense another sentient life which has a high psi. An adept will convince that psi-rated person that life on Edain will enhance psychic capabilities—which it will, or so the Guild maintains.

"Those dreamweavers throughout the UOoP, however, are incapable of complete incarnation when spinning their yarns. A seventh level weaver can spin so precisely the characters lose the transparency of a holograph, and look and feel like flesh and blood. In fact, they speak their parts. A weaver's voice is inaudible. There is even speculation, unconfirmed by dreamweavers, an adept could maintain a thread at distance."

Tine wondered what that would be like, imagined what a Caliban fabler might do during an elderlatch when broods would gather and hear the history of their people spun out into the night. And that was a stimulating thought to Tine. Of all the arts, spinning was the one which most fascinated him, and for a Caliban, that excitement manifested during elderlatch in an abandon of coupling, where, as with the first feast of the rains, resulted in feasting of another kind until you puked and then feasted some more. Aganth had been right. He did want a dreamweaver. It was just the way of a Caliban.

He stilled his instincts. "You think a character, a thread, replaced a person?"

"If a powerful enough weaver spun the thread, it's possible."

"How does a character—"

"Die? It vanishes. That's what happened to my Active."

"Was the Active important?"

"To me."

"Who was she?"

"My daughter." Jabod's eyes glittered. "That's another reason I'm sending you, Tine—because of your hunter instincts. I know you'll serve both my purposes. The other reason, the official reason? You're the only one above suspicion. Who is going to suspect a Caliban who has never been involved in anything outside of Setebos? And you're the only one I can be sure hasn't been replaced by a thread—a weaver character."

Which again caused Tine to consider what had been presented to him. How was he to identify who or what was and wasn't real? He asked Jabod that. There was no answer, at least nothing Tine could use. And that in turn caused him to question if even Jabod was who he was purported to be. Or what about the crew on this liner? The captain? Anyone, for that matter? If skilled dreamweavers were so adept at creating threads which could replace real individuals, who exactly was Tine to trust, and what exactly was the real situation here?

"Am I to be escorted when I land?"

"The Guild members will meet you." He touched

the disc on his wrist and drew a rectangle on the table. Figures sprang out of the rectangle.

"They are the Edain Guild," he said, gesturing to the figures. "One elected representative from each of the arts. This," and he pointed to a squat figure who looked like a giant aloe, "is Tylan, Master Sculptor. His particular medium is light, and his particular weakness is anger. This one needs care.

"To his right is Hogan, the Master Photographer—arcane art, that; Jan the Master Holographer; Athran the Master Painter, and this," he indicated a humanoid female, "is Ela, Master Dreamweaver. The other sixty are all Masters of their fields, but these five are those with whom you will be concerned. Especially Ela." Jabod isolated the five figures with a gesture, and fingered them up in size. "Hogan and Jan are inseparable, and what one thinks the other concurs. Both are extremely clever, twins, lovers in fact. Athran, on the other hand, plays the part of the shit-disturber and likes it. It's hard to tell when he's playing or when he's serious. Use discretion with that one.

"Ela will be your focus. She didn't get to be Master Dreamweaver for nothing. Her fame as a weaver is unprecedented and her power with the Guild to be acknowledged.

"Politically, we know nothing about them. IPCIB's never been able to get a grant out of the UOoP to place an Active on Edain. That's your job—to gather information for us." Jabod flicked the figures away. "By the way, you needn't worry about clothing conformities. The Edains are going to want to paint you, sculpt you, photograph you, holograph you, and whatever else they can think of."

Tine stiffened. "I hadn't thought about it."

Jabod grinned. "I know. That's what I like about you."

"How am I going to convince them that an envoy to Setebos will survive spore invasion?"

"We've developed a synthetic spore which is going to open your planet to travel. You'll be able to return to your family."

He didn't respond to the latter. Why tell Jabod that he'd left in disgrace, divorced? But, then, if IPCIB had been monitoring him, Jabod already knew.

"That should be convincing," he answered.

"That's up to you. You can access all this information through your implant." Jabod stood. "Good luck." He strode away before Tine could say anything else.

Tine looked down at the tiny disk in his wrist, wondering for what he'd need luck. He wasn't even sure he could handle this mission. A problem like this needed a seasoned Active, not some bumpkin from an isolated planet. What did he know about subterfuge? About political games? About the arts? Perhaps it was for these reasons Jabod wished him luck. Tine was a poor choice at best. It would be better if he went back to Setebos now, gave his apologies to Jabod, risked incurring the wrath of IPCIB.

I can go back, he thought. What for?

There was nothing for him now but this mission. Somehow he'd have to find a life in that.

ENTERING THE Edain nebula was something Tine
was sure he'd never forget. He'd studied this gas
cloud, enchanted by veils of red and gold, purple and
blue. But once the IPCIB liner slipped dimensions
and re-emerged in the Edain nebula, that spectacle
vanished. It was just space. Black and white. Gone
were the enormous veils of colour from clouds of
gas and debris. There was no Eye of God, no Tower
of Colossus. He felt cheated by his disappointment,
by the hard truth of reality. It occurred to him some
things were beautiful only at a distance.

And so he turned his face away from the nebula he'd
dreamed of entering. He'd wanted to be surrounded
in colour, to experience that grandeur, for it to last
and be something more than transition; but instead
it was more like fleeting memory than something
real. He was accustomed to long periods of stillness
in his life, of the ability to experience grandeur and
scope, to know that tomorrow and tomorrow this
colour, this sweep of majesty would be there, until
time had passed in a languorous progression. And

then change, sudden and startling, which then ebbed into another languorous progression. On Setebos, there was an amber landscape, shading to madder red and sienna browns. And when flora erupted there was a riot of green and red, colours beyond embracing until you became so accustomed to colour it seemed uninteresting. Then the slow slide back into a sere and spiritual scene.

He drew a rectangle in the air with a finger, muttered, "Screen," and watched that space haze. "Edain capitol," he said and watched a real-time feed bloom in that rectangle.

Where Setebos had been a study of simplicity, even of illusion, what now appeared before him was a writhing, blinding, completely alien landscape. There was nothing subtle here, none of the tone upon tone that made up his home. Setebos was all open spaces. Every day was different to the next and the next, different in a way only a Caliban could appreciate. Flower one day. None the next. Fruit the following. Even colours changed with this same rhythm. Dun to taupe, taupe to cream, cream to peach, peach to rose, and on so that with first dawn a new mood infused the land. But now his eyes stung with a torrent of colours. Setebos had nothing like this. He'd never seen all colours hurled together at once, unmodified, raw in their primary essence. It was painful. Offensive. Perverted. He could think of no other way to perceive this. Everything shouted ersatz, contrived.

He felt a growing sense of disappointment, of disillusionment.

The people! So many people! How could they live

like this, body upon body, jostling just to make headway?

Claustrophobia seized him. He shuddered, afraid of what the tastes, textures, and smells of this place would do to him, thinking himself a fool for having desired this. The last thing he wanted was to appear the back-planet bumpkin, and in a place like this he could be little else.

And yet there was a paradise of knowledge nestled into this orgy of sensation. He wondered at the logic of it, of the danger of becoming so absorbed in sensation you could drown. There were Caliban stories of the *gulous,* the Caliban-become-beast who consumed the world. Was he in danger of courting that myth, of transforming into legend and becoming outcast, of destroying everything that mattered in his life?

It occurred to him he was already an outcast. Was it possible he'd forsaken his own paradise? It was too absurd to contemplate.

An overhead light warned him to prepare for docking. He wiped the rectangle of information and it dissolved. How would he do Jabod justice on this mission? He had no idea how to respond to what he'd just seen. He'd thought he'd be captivated. Instead he felt captive.

Why send him?

He hopped off the stool, massaging the glands under his arms and without thinking rubbed oil across his chest and hips. He looked down at what he'd done, turned up his hands to look at the pads on his palms. They glistened.

Would the Edains even understand him? He was

to transport to Edain alone, arriving at the capitol, Maxta. Jabod was to stay aboard, posing as safe passage. The Commissioner warned him of Edain's half-Setebos gravity and rich hydrogen atmosphere. Breathing would be difficult. He would adjust, he'd been told. He'd been told as long as he stayed within the domed regions he'd be safe. Twenty-four hours UOoP, thirty chronoms Setebos—that had been how long it would take for him to feel comfortable. It has been the same adjustment period as leaving Setebos.

That did nothing to calm him. He'd been so sure he wanted to escape from Setebos, from the rituals which were a part of life with Aganth and his brood.

He trotted to the disembarkation portal, nodded to Jabod and the tech who operated the run. Now, watching the shimmering cylinder of the run, he wondered if he'd really wanted escape, or merely wanted to taste something new. Aganth and his brood wound through his memory as tightly as the spore once had. To just walk away from a lifetime of familiarity wasn't as painless as he'd thought. There were so many things he should have said to her. So many moments he should have marked. How was he to navigate in this now? There was no experience from which to draw. Only instinct. And instinct told him beware.

Tine nodded to Jabod, an indication he was prepared—*liar!*—fidgeting with memory, bristling with instinct. He watched Jabod closely, reading signs, respirations, being the hunter in terrain not to his liking.

Jabod's gaze swung round the room, the floating screens, the reports, over to Tine. "Ready?"

"Yes." He hoped the lie would cover itself. For him it would be like starting all over again. Nothing would be familiar.

"Good. They're all going to be too interested in what your planet's like. Edain's a study of excess. You come from a place of simplicity. They'll find that fascinating—a new expression of creativity."

"What if I want to contact you?"

"We've uploaded a program change to your implant. Just say my name and it will patch you through to me. We've also added a GPS so we can locate you."

Tine growled, looked at the disk in his wrist. "GPS so you'll know where I am."

"We could have loaded a program that would let us know every fart you make."

Had Jabod watched Tine's withdrawal? Moreover, had Jabod listened to the exchange Tine had with his unknown medics? Suddenly now Tine wondered if he weren't the lure in this hunt?

Jabod motioned to the run. "It's time to go."

If that was meant to put Tine at ease, it didn't. What's more, Tine felt as though he were going to be the latest circus act to amuse the Edains. At that moment, he felt the spore had isolated him in more ways than he realized. Living on Setebos ill-prepared him for the attention of off-worlders.

His hooves thumped loudly on the cushioned floor as he crossed to the shimmering light of the run, which reached out like hands to grasp and pull him through time and dimension and deposit him once again in this reality but in a different place. Something screamed in his chest.

He attached his attention to the light, thinking of Aganth, thinking of Setebos. He felt the oiliness of his hide. Afraid? Yes, afraid. Would he make a fool of himself also?

He glanced at Jabod.

"Ready?"

Tine nodded. Another step put him at the precipice of the luminous shaft. Something inside him spun through a cartwheel. It was lunacy to step into that glowing hole. He glanced at Jabod, and then skipped his attention over to the tech. They gave him a thumbs-up sign.

As a matter of pride, he committed his hide to this wonder of physics. The moment his hoof entered the light he was captured. He stiffened, fell. Wind howled over his body, hot, terrible. A scream ripped from his throat. Instructions flashed through his head. He relaxed. His fall arrested. It was like rocking in a womb of brilliance. With a toothy grin, Tine decided dimension slipping was a welcome mode of transportation. Second time was easier than the first.

His euphoria was short-lived. Within moments he was aware of polished stone beneath his hooves—slick and dangerous to someone like him. What purchase would his hooves have on this surface?

That was when he realized he felt light, somehow taller. The lack of gravity added to his precarious hold. He inhaled, coughing. Giddiness swept over him. It took everything he knew to stop from giggling.

In an attempt at orientation, he peered through the curtain of light. Although he was aware of an arc of bodies and shapes, faces and dress were unidentifiable.

Carefully, he stepped out of the light. He felt his hoof slide, followed by his leg, and with a loud thump he landed on his fleshy rump. Pain shot up his back. Mortified, he tried to stand. It was impossible to gain purchase on the plaza of purple crystal. Again and again he slid. Laughter percolated around him.

Resigned to his humiliation, Tine remained where he'd sprawled, confronting the welcoming committee. A rapid count made him realize the entire Guild, all sixty of them, had come to receive him, a few of whom were tittering behind their hands, or what served as hands. Something in their mannerisms said they were laughing at him, not with him.

He stifled a growl.

Movement from a woman caught his attention. It was hard to get a fix on her. Something about her was almost nebulous, unidentifiable. Two beings at her side stepped forward, assisting Tine to his feet. She smiled dreamily.

"We weren't informed you were adept at the art of humour, Ambassador Tine," she said. "What a grand entrance. Welcome."

Tine managed to keep his balance once he was upright, although he was unsure how controlled that would be if he moved. He nodded to her welcome.

"I'm Ela," she said, "Master Dreamweaver. We'll leave introductions until later, if that meets with your approval." She didn't wait to receive it. "I'll escort you to your suite, and let you settle." She glanced around. "Your luggage?"

He grinned, gesturing to his body. "For what would I need luggage?"

Ela's gaze cooled, slipping over Tine.

He caught the reaction of the two beings who had assisted him and then those from the remainder of the entourage. What was it he read in them? Ridicule? Surprise? Curiosity? How could you read anything from such a host of alien life forms? What might mean laughter to one might be a matter for umbrage to another. Was that a smile? How did a flora-based sentience express itself? Or what about that puddle of ochre jelly? Oh, look at that, it changes colour. Is that like a cephalopod, expressing itself through a change in light spectrum? He questioned more and more the wisdom of sending him in to do this job, and that was when he wondered if his earlier speculation weren't correct, that he was a pawn in a larger game. The sacrificial piece. Bait.

Again Ela made a gesture, her hand pale, long-fingered. Tine thought of the filament spider of Setebos, the way it seemed to glide more than walk on legs like gossamer. A floater path sprang into existence under him, raising his body above the treacherous crystal. He was pleased he didn't flinch.

"Are you familiar with floaters?" she asked.

"From second-hand knowledge. But as I don't know where we're going, I'll let you think us there."

She nodded.

The path brought him fluidly to Ela's side, where she joined him. He'd achieved one movement without teetering into collapse, assisted as it might have been. It did everything to restore his confidence.

At Ela's direction, the remainder of the Guild boarded and their conveyance expanded as necessary. It was plain as a shout to him who influenced the Guild. Ela was the master of Masters. Standing beside her, he was sure even he would fall thrall to her power.

Movement overcame him once more, as the path carried the entourage across the crowded plaza. Just ahead floated a free-form sculpture which shifted colours so subtly it was like watching a setting sun. This was something he could appreciate.

That was when Tine became aware of the lack of warmth on his hide. The air wasn't cool. But neither was it rich with a sun's rays. He looked up. There was one disk of white up there. But there was no heat. He frowned.

"I thought Edain was in a tight orbit of this star?" he said.

"It is," Ela replied.

"You're shielding?"

"The domes which enclose our cities aren't enough."

"I wasn't aware there was enough radiation to be harmful."

"There isn't."

"Then why shield?"

"Diffused light is better for artistic endeavour. It doesn't create hot and cool spots which can destroy expression."

"What about visual artists?"

She frowned. "Contrast can be created artificially. It gives our visual artists better control. All of us approve of the screening as it allows forty-two hours a day of even light."

"No night?" He couldn't imagine not having night. It had been a time heralded by songs, warmed by scented fires, smiles around a mat where the first evening meal of ripe grain, vegetables and nutmeats would be shared. The brood would settle after third supper. He and Aganth would walk under five moons, find the bower of sand and rock and again share the pleasures of mates.

How could they not have night?

"No night," she answered. "We create around the clock if we wish. If a night situation is required, we simply simulate. The conditions are most ideal for our gardeners. You can imagine what success they have."

Even so, it seemed deformed to him. "What about heat? That's controlled too?"

"Indeed. We have no wish to fry like—" She inhaled sharply. "Why be hot when you can be comfortable?"

Tine could only indicate his understanding with a gesture; to comment would have enhanced Ela's disdain and his confusion. Had that comment she'd almost made been in reference to him, or something she was hiding? Would he have been enlightened?

By now their direction took them on a collision course with the sculpture. His body was so slick with oil he wondered he wasn't growling. But then he did growl when they passed right through the sculpture. Laughter erupted behind him.

Ela smiled that distant smile. "Didn't you realize the sculpture is one of Master Tylan's works?"

Tine shook his head. "On Setebos, we sculpt with the land, with solid materials."

"Then we have a great deal to learn from one another."

His mission wasn't foremost in his mind when he answered, "Yes, we have a lot to learn."

For the remainder of the journey, Tine wrapped himself in silence and observation. Nothing in the images and feeds could have prepared him for this. There seemed to be no rules, as was evident even in the architecture. Unconventional materials were used for building. Few were opaque. Many were entirely glass rather than a composite—unthinkable—some of crystals; there were even a few created from precious gems. The more mundane were of composites or what appeared to be earthen materials not unlike his own home. The wealth of the planet was flaunted with such abandon he almost became numb to it.

When he came to an area where people seemingly floated innumerable floors above him, he grasped an image of how wealthy Edain had become. What kind of expenditure in power did it take to create such a tower out of nothing but gravitational manipulation?

Tine's memory filled with a dun-coloured adobe hut that hugged the land of Setebos like the carcass of a worm. He shrank into that memory.

By the time Ela halted him inside a green clay building, he was completely unhinged. He hadn't realized the rest of the entourage disappeared earlier on. How was it his native instincts hadn't warned him, hadn't informed him? His gaze fired up to Ela who stood four heads above him. She smiled that inscrutable smile.

"Your journey has wearied you, Ambassador Tine."

He nodded, averse to using his voice.

She continued through gates, a courtyard dripping with bloom and vegetation and the tintinnabulation of water, through an arch toward a lift, her tone mild and sleepy. "I would suggest a good soak and a nap before twenty-thirty. You're to be our guest of honour tonight."

He made no reply to that. Why would they want him in a place of honour?

After the short ascent in a smaller version of the IPCIB liner's transporter, they stepped onto a thickly carpeted floor of silver-grey, and halted before one of three doors. To the right of the entrance was a square hole, rimmed with some type of light-emitting substance.

Ela nodded to the hole. "If you'll be so kind as to place your hand in there."

He stiffened.

"It's security, Ambassador Tine."

Awash with foolishness, Tine did as he was asked. The bands of light erupted into brilliance, but nothing occurred within the chamber. He withdrew his hand, turning it over, back, frowning.

"Don't you have security locks on Setebos?"

The door swung open.

His gaze shot up.

"No...no locks of any kind."

"How odd." She waved him to enter.

The suite was simply accoutered, a sleeping room, a hygiene room, and another he assumed was where people gathered to eat and sing evening songs. The latter, however, was furnished with straight-backed seats, stiff, uncompromising. Each room had a scene-window which belied the buildings on which his suite faced. The vistas were of rain-forests, space-scapes and exotic aquatic gardens. Why hide the architecture?

Ela hovered in the entrance.

"If you have any needs, Ambassador Tine, just speak." She laughed. He shuddered with pleasure. "You could say the walls have ears. I'll be back at twenty to escort you to the Plaza Orchid. It's where a festival in your honour is being held."

As before, she didn't wait to receive his consent. The door closed. He glanced around, feeling a prisoner, or more to the point a specimen caught in a bubble. Although he was alone, he felt he'd never be allowed the privilege of isolation while he was here. She had said the walls had ears. Was that more than services built into the walls? Was he, in fact, being watched? And as he wondered about that he remembered that journey from the run to this suite, how it was Edains seemed to be forever at spectacle. Everything was a studied composition. And staring at these foreign surroundings, he realized he was to be part of that composition, that spectacle.

IT OCCURRED to Tine he'd stood at the edge of the bath, staring, thinking, for a very long time. There were rust-coloured tiles, ornately painted with flora beyond his imagining, feathered and winged creatures diving through leaves as though toying with unseen marine life. At the drain were the black stamens of a blue flower, petals tissue-thin. Even in paint the flower was fragile. It occurred to him the bath was the only elaborate thing in the entire suite.

He remembered Setebos. Baths were part of ritual there, ceremonies performed for beginnings and endings: beginnings of two lives to be lived together; endings of lives well-lived. To bathe wasn't something done out of mere whim.

Tine wondered if he should bathe in acknowledgement of a life past.

That idea didn't fit the confusion of these past few days. Aganth was still on Setebos. That life wasn't past. Divorced he might be, but to cancel those years with Aganth, years built upon ritual and familiarity, would be the same as divorcing himself. It was then he confronted the fact Aganth was still a part of his life, and so to bathe in dismissal would be false. He flinched.

But then why would Ela wish him to bathe? He distinctly remembered her saying he would have time to bathe and prepare before attending the banquet. Prepare what? A speech? Himself? Was there danger for which he need be prepared? Most certainly that, but whether the danger was life-threatening or merely challenging remained to be discovered, and he realized he had no information, nothing by which he could guide his actions. At that point he wondered if all IPCIB's operatives were so starved of information. Had Jabod been entirely forthcoming? Or was Tine being used as part of a greater hunt? The fact he hadn't considered that previously was unsettling, reinforcing his growing awareness: Aganth had likely been right about more than one point.

Fool, he most likely was.

Too late now.

He looked to the mirrors surrounding the bath. He was unsure of the thing staring at him. Would they think him grotesque, ghoulish, a sentience entombed inside a nightmare? Would they think him beautiful, exotic, find wonder in the arrangement of his cells? And why would that matter? Why had all the holos he'd been fed so preoccupied with what others thought, about what might, nor might not, be considered beautiful? Maybe there was a reason mirrors were rare on Setebos. He backed, pivoted, his hooves clicking on the warm-toned wood. Bathing wasn't important now.

When he entered the space where he was supposed to sleep, he decided to deny rest as well. This entire preoccupation with furniture to accommodate sleeping, sitting, eating, all reinforced the fact he was alien to this world, to these requirements of civilization. Was he, then, considered uncivilized because of his species' habits? Was it necessary to have all these *things* to be considered intelligent, worthy of consideration as a political and economic entity? Did the fact his bed on Setebos consisted of a packed earthen platform make him and his kind no better than a herd animal raised for meat or milk?

What made a species civilized? What was civilization?

Esoteric thought, he muttered to himself. Nonsense and unnecessary, and so he continued to trot into a larger space. He asked the walls: "What is this space?"

"Define space."

"This space where I'm standing, this enclosure—what is it?"

"The main salon."

He thought about that, looked around. "What is its purpose?"

"A place to meet with guests."

He thought about that, about what was apparently a custom to set aside enclosed spaces for needs other than shelter. But then perhaps it wasn't so much a custom as a reaction to a planet apparently hostile to life. Or life as the UOoP knew it. What was beyond the domes? Surely something. Something quite other than this manufactured world in which he found himself.

He was insulating himself against the indulgences Edain's domes offered, he realized, as if to ignore his surroundings was to deny his discomfort. How could he possibly do IPCIB any good here? He knew nothing but Caliban ritual. What did he know of gathering facts?

You were sent on a mission, he thought. *Facts better be your first concern.*

And so, standing in another foreign room, surrounded by objects he didn't understand, he sank to his haunches and turned to facts. The brief he'd been given said the Edains lived solely for artistic expression. Everything else, including simple economic realities, seemed unimportant and alien to their way of life, and so all food production, service, support and manufacturing industries that allowed an individual to exist were contracted out. The brief had not elaborated who or what fulfilled those contracts. Yet certainly there had to be a huge industrial and commercial base here in order to support Edain's considerable domed population. It couldn't all be brought in from off-world.

It was then he realized the absence of any such areas both in his brief on Edain. There had been nothing visible in any of the satellite imagery he'd studied, and certainly during the memorable trip from his landing to this shelter there had been no evidence of even the simplest of commerce. He understood many cultures and species conducted business through what were known as street vendors, basically itinerant traders, to both hawk wares and noshables, and often offer services.

But there had been nothing. Just a xeno-cultural press of bodies, of language, of noise and activity all against a backdrop of architecture that tried too hard to achieve new dimensions of artistic expression.

Where were their areas of agriculture? How did they feed all these people? Or were they a hunter-gatherer society? He didn't see how they could be, how they could support such a population the way Setebos did.

Which brought him again to the questions: *What's outside the domes?*

But then why wouldn't something show up on satellite imagery? Was it that these necessary fields of existence were concealed from his preliminary tour within this dome? Or was it that these commonplace industries were concealed from the artists who were the ruling party because those industries were considered ugly? But how could that be? Certainly there were many industries necessary to existence that could be considered art. What about culinary art? And what about all the ancillary industries that fed those industries? Were they not, by extension, also art? Wasn't a job well done art?

When did art become ugly? Perhaps he was hyper-sensitive? Over-reacting? Over-thinking?

He twitched, growled, looked around his surroundings once again.

"Can I change my surroundings?" he asked aloud.

"Yes," said the air.

He growled again, uncomfortable with this unseen,

unknown intelligence. "Do you know what Caliban shelter looks like?"

"Yes."

"Can you make this space look like that?"

"Yes."

"Will it feel just like the real thing?"

"Of course."

"Why?"

"Because it will be the real thing."

"How?"

"We manipulate matter."

What did that mean? How could they manipulate matter? But then wasn't that what every artist did? Manipulate matter? What did a potter do but manipulate mud into a vessel of grace and functionality? Did not a glass-blower combine base sands and subject them to heat to create liquid to create a more stable liquid that disguised itself as solid? Wasn't every form of art a metamorphosis? Was life, then, art?

And how to ask the intelligence that spoke to him from the air any of this?

He'd watch, he decided. He had the feeling if he asked questions he'd receive no answers, all part of the illusory nature of this mercurial society.

That had been plain enough when Ela evaded direct questions during his brief encounter. It would surprise him not at all if she deliberately guided him around any areas considered sensitive.

But, then, perhaps the banquet would provide a few leads?

His next concern was whether he had to occupy himself for awhile, or if Ela would arrive shortly. She had said she would return at twenty.

Twenty, he thought. *Twenty what? Twenty breaths? Twenty paces? Twenty chronoms? How do they measure a life?*

Again, he felt unprepared for this mission. There had been so little time.

"What time is it?" he asked the air.

Time to eat? Time to sleep? Time to fornicate?

"It's now eighteen."

He barked a laugh. "Convert two hours Edain time to two chronoms Setebos time."

There was no answer for a few moments, then: "Two hours Edain equals four point three chronoms Setebos."

Already he itched with boredom.

"Thank you," he mumbled, and glanced at the door. Faced with either snoring away this block of time, or slurping culture, he plodded his way into the bewilderment of this cosmopolitan planet. Better to learn from the natives, than to learn from government officials preoccupied with deception, because he was convinced there would be nothing but deception in what he'd be shown.

When he gained the hotel entrance, he paused, milling in the hubbub while studying other pedestrians. There was every assortment of sentient being in the collage before him: descendants from reptiles, avians and mammalians; things which looked like ochre squish, lumbering rocks and frantic insects. Among these, those which piqued his curiosity were things which were obviously plant and yet equally mobile and sentient. He remembered Tylan, the Master Sculptor. There lay another rendezvous he longed to make. Tylan, he was sure, could afford him enlightenment. That much had been clear in the scant information he'd received on the IPCIB liner. Everything they suspected had been revealed through Tylan's angry outbursts.

He glanced around again, decided he would blend well enough in this cornucopia.

His next problem lay in mobility. He had no desire to test his hooves on the dome's avenues. That had already been indelibly imprinted on his pride. What to do? Few street travellers were actually pedestrians. Most drifted around on floater-paths, a system of transportation which required knowledge of a particular destination. Tine didn't know of a destination.

He almost despaired use of some sentient vehicle when a litter popped into existence. A blast of wind hit him. It took the time Tine used to regain his balance to realize the sudden gust of air had been created by something which had moved at either high speed, or some form of a vacuum being filled. He stared narrowly at the whimsy before him.

The litter was really what appeared to be a fringed rug, intricate in design, and brazen in colour. Red was the predominant hue, a red so bright it was almost bloody. But there were indigo blues scattered at random, golds which paled to anaemic beiges, and black like ink-work scrawling across it.

"Where are we going, Ambassador?" something squeaked.

Tine swallowed. His gaze shot to his right. There, atop this hovering rug was a…. He wasn't sure what it was. It was as leathery, brown and warty as he, eyes like onyx, feet which ended in talons, which, in turn, pierced the rug, appendages Tine could only assume were arms, and a simian face.

"Are we going somewhere?" he asked.

He watched as the thing's body quivered. Obviously, it hadn't been prepared for his composure, although composed wasn't what he felt. Everything unhinged his perspective. Nothing, so far, gave him any common reference, anything he could identify and say, yes, I know that.

"I assumed you wanted to explore."

"And you know what I want to do?"

"Shouldn't I?"

He ignored that. It was a question he was unprepared to examine. Already he felt as if he couldn't assimilate anything else. Overload. So much newness! How could he absorb all this?

He looked back over his surroundings. "And you know how to get around."

His own strangeness rankled once more, and desperate to identify his place in this world, he acquiesced to adventure.

"How do I board this—"

"Transport?" The creature giggled. "Just sit on it."

Tine did that. Softness surrounded him, not something that made him particularly comfortable. He was aware he was rubbing oil into his hide.

"Now what?" he asked, watching as he was watched by passersby. Just another part of the spectacle.

"Tell me what you'd like to do."

Tine thought about that. He hadn't considered what, exactly, he was going to do once loose on the streets. The only thing he had considered was his belly. It had been awhile since last he ate. An intolerable situation. At least two meals had gone unsatisfied.

"I'm hungry."

"But your banquet is at—"

"We Calibans eat a lot. I'm hungry."

The creature rippled its leathery hide, blinked and sank its talons deeper into the rug. "As you wish."

A desperate feeling of non-being swallowed him. He could sense nothing, see nothing, hear nothing, smell nothing. What he did feel was fear. At the same moment he realized how foolish he'd been to commit his hide to some bizarre, unknown mode of transport. This had not been in any of the material in his briefing. Was he so smitten with the planet that he'd ignore common sense? It was possible that whatever element had caused the deception with the Gelt Ambassador might use him as well, and now here he was, falling through whatever was happening to him, like some beast tethered for slaughter. Instinct told him to leap away from the rug, from the creature who had taken them into whatever this no-place was, but to where would he leap? And what then? Would he survive? Would he know where he was? And just when he was sure he'd have to throttle his guide into submission, sensation once again spilled over him.

His first reaction was to brilliant light, his inner eyelids nictitating. The creature giggled. He inhaled sharply. Smells smacked him. Protein. Blood. He turned toward the source of that seduction, purring, forgetting his momentary caution.

"Go! Go!" his guide cackled. "I'll wait here."

Tine didn't think when he slid off the rug and trotted into the space before him. At that moment he was aware of nothing but the scents of succulent food. He had no idea where he was, the condition of his surroundings, or even of other beings. All he could think of was the tune Aganth hummed while preparing his natal feast. That had been many years ago, before his involvement in IPCIB. He remembered Aganth sang often. And he remembered that he'd harmonized with her on evenings in the dry season, when their voices softened the harshness of the landscape.

When he entered the space, the smells were liquid. He salivated. Somebody rushed up to him, mumbled something about a table, and, mechanically, Tine nodded, following where the person led. It seemed such an odd thing—to have a building dedicated to eating. This was something he knew only from holos.

Some time had passed before he felt sufficiently sated, an array of empty vessels around him. But the entire time he'd been aware of where he was, and the other beings who had come and gone. It wouldn't do to feed in a strange place and drop his guard. Calibans died forgetting that rule on Setebos, especially when hauling home a large kill for a brood. He tried to find the command to clear his table, but realized it was a holographic solid, same with the chairs. He watched a waiter attend a party of patrons, caught the appearance of a seating arrangement to accommodate the various needs of the poly-xeno trio. Had the waiter sub-vocalized a command? And why was every single waiter a humanoid not unlike Ela? Nothing about them indicated anything like android behaviour. Clones? Were Edains expressing art through embryo manipulation? And why was it most other patrons ignored the waiters as if they didn't exist or weren't worthy of notice?

He beckoned to one of the servers, aware it was custom here to exchange currency for service, and when he received the response: "Oh, no need, Ambassador Tine. You're Edain's guest," he became acutely aware the server, like the others, seemed dreamlike, as though listening to something else while functioning here.

That act of welcome did nothing but make Tine feel unwelcome. He was almost positive he'd interpreted the social custom correctly, felt insulted his attempt to fit into Edain society had been thwarted, that they made special accommodation for him. He grunted, rose and lumbered for the door. It wasn't until then he realized he'd been saved an embarrassing moment, because he had no idea how he would have transacted an exchange of remuneration. He had no currency, no funds from which to draw even had he known how to link into some form of payment gateway. That his cultural and economic necessity had been overlooked in his briefing set off more alarms, and suddenly he was aware there was nothing about this mission approaching what he assumed was IPCIB normal.

How could Jabod send in an Active without any way to transact business? Even on Setebos a regulated form of barter took place. You knew the worth of goods or services to be traded, and what equivalents were acceptable.

But at least now he knew it was likely currency wasn't to be a problem. Still, it rankled.

Outside, as promised, his rug was waiting. Tine's head spun with questions when he boarded. It was still spinning when he popped back in front of the hotel, gasping from yet another excursion through whatever temporal displacement he'd been dragged through. He sat there a moment on the rug, staring at his guide, measuring the way it breathed, the way it watched both him and its surroundings, seemingly a part of and detached from everything. Alien. Even on this planet peopled by aliens this thing was alien. He knew it. He felt it.

"What are you?" he finally asked.

"What am I?" the creature squeaked. It seemed nonplussed. "What do you want me to be?"

"Honest."

"Honest... honest...hm-m-m, well, yes.... I'm a thread."

There was something about that term he should remember. What was a thread? He reiterated that question aloud.

"Oh, don't be dense! You know, a thread, part of a tapestry!"

Tine remembered the bath, the problem with time.

Words, words, words....

"Of course," he mumbled. "And I'm a warp. It's all very clear."

"Exactly! Oh, I'm so glad!" And the guide popped out of existence.

Thread? Tapestry? Warp?

Tine spun around and thumped into the hotel lobby, ignoring the greetings from the desk clerk who was, as before, quite detached, and yet quite aware. On the way up the lift, something about the desk clerk reminded him of the waiters in the bistro. He couldn't quite identify it, but something was meshing, or rather, not meshing.

He grinned. *This is one big mesh!*

He stepped into his hallway and attempted to open his door. When the handle remained inoperative, he remembered the security lock. He slid his hand into the hole. The door sprang open. He entered.

Another piece of the puzzle, he thought. If they were all such a group of dedicated artists, with no crime, and an egalitarian society, why did they need locks? What were they trying to protect?

Slowly, he sank to his haunches in the foyer. His claws, he realized, had unsheathed. He stared at them, at the gold connectivity paint that allowed him access to his own information portal. Was his data safe? Would it be monitored? By whom?

It was then he thought: Or, like me, from whom are they trying to protect themselves?

WHERE HE was now seemed an impossibility, and Jabod struggled with the concept, struggled with the fact he'd slipped through time and space by means of the manipulation of a woman he'd thought a gifted storyteller.

None of this sat right with Jabod. Not the problem with the Gelt Ambassador, his daughter, this mission, and now being here on Edain with Ela. Nothing.

Should he have sent in Tine? Probably not. Tine was too inexperienced, too unfamiliar with the way of things outside Setebos. But who else was there to trust? Tine was the only one who hadn't been contaminated by the outside world. There was no risk the Guild had contacted Tine before him.

Even so, how would Tine know if something weren't right? Was it good enough to rely on the Caliban's hunter instinct? Would Tine's instinct be alarm enough in the face of political subterfuge?

He paced a square in the space to which Ela had brought him, a nebulous place of clouds, sensing the wrongness of everything around him, damning himself for overlooking something so completely crucial that it would jeopardize Tine's operation. Ela. How could he have so grossly misjudged her? And how the hell had she managed to fold time and space, violate all the physical laws of the universe and just swim through the run as though it were her own personal highway?

All of the facts had been reviewed and reviewed, and still Jabod could find nothing. Proof of that lay in the holos he'd drawn around himself.

The same questions occurred to him: Why create a clone and then have that clone dissolve? Why go to such an elaborate ruse only to have it fail? Why risk so much on such an imperfect sham?

Why?

He sank to the edge of the cloud that formed his sleeping platform, cradling his head in his hands. The air seemed to compress and then he heard a pop. A diminutive ball of a creature appeared before him.

"Master Ela wishes to see you," it said, baring teeth in what he assumed was a smile. It let out a cackle.

His gaze shot to the clouds that contained him in this place. "Master Ela?"

"She's waiting for your permission to speak with you."

Permission? He wanted to laugh at the absurdity of it. Here was a person who had effortlessly created a double of him and just as effortlessly swept him out and away. All he knew was that he was likely on Edain, but where, exactly, he had no idea. And now she wanted his permission to speak with him? As if she had to ask? As if he had the power to deny her anything?

But the niceties had to be met. "Tell her I'll see her."

The creature winked out of existence. Jabod's senses switched on. Why would Master Ela wish to see him? Was there something wrong with Tine?

His unease reached a climax when Ela stepped through the clouds. He was aware of her power. It swam about her like her own atmosphere—real, intoxicating, somehow dangerous.

"What brings you here?" he asked, remaining where he sat.

"I think we've found the Gelt Ambassador."

Now that was a surprise. "Where?"

"There's been a communication from the rebels. They say—"

"Rebels?"

"They aren't a faction the Guild chooses to acknowledge." Jabod arched a brow. "We have an anti-Guild faction on Edain. An annoyance, really. They tend to disrupt our service and manufacturing industries."

"Why haven't you told IPCIB? That's what we're here for."

"There hasn't been any need. We're perfectly capable of handling this ourselves."

"I disagree. The Gelt Ambassador wouldn't have gone missing if you had any control."

"We argue a moot point."

"What the Guild has done is a major infraction—"

"Let's not get caught up in technicalities."

"Technicalities? I hardly think a rebel uprising, one that plainly has one or more dreamweavers, can be dismissed as a technicality."

Her eyes narrowed. "What makes you think dreamweavers are involved?"

"Don't play me for a fool. It was plain enough dreamweavers were involved when the Gelt Ambassador's body dissolved before our eyes, the way a dreamweaver character dissolves. I wasn't about to believe that had been the real Ambassador. And then there's my double."

"So dreamweavers are involved."

"That's enough for me to put the entire planet under martial law."

"Are you going to mouth me threats, or are you going to help to investigate this claim about the Gelt Ambassador?"

He hissed, exasperated with the way she stood there, so cool, aloof, untouchable. Her kind were the hardest to crack. Little penetrated. "What do you want from me?"

"The rebels have requested you attend a meeting."

"What kind of meeting?"

"To arrange for the release of the Gelt Ambassador."

"A ransom?"

"It didn't sound like ransom to me. I think they just want to be heard."

"What makes you think I'll agree to the meeting?"

She smiled. "You wouldn't want to risk the ire of the Gelt Consortium."

Match point. He couldn't argue that. All that

wealth. All that commerce. Still, knowing did nothing to allay his fears and suspicions. But what choice did he have? "I'll go."

"They've asked it be covert."

"You really must think me a fool if you assume I'll agree to that."

She shrugged. "That's their demand."

"There has to be some other way."

"None."

He stiffened. Was she one of the rebels? Had he been so blind? But how else to find out what happened to the Gelt Ambassador? Tine might never have this opportunity. Or maybe they already had him.

Jabod stood, aware he had no power here, said as much to her. Ela smiled. It was then his nightmare began.

TINE HAD fingered open a screen when he'd arrived back in his suite, and since then he'd been involved in analysing existing security codes and implementing his own. He wasn't going to take any chances. There were details he wished to store and consider later, details about his trip out in Edain's streets. Over and over he'd asked himself if the character on the rug had been real. It seemed real enough, but the way it had known what he wanted left him speculating.

If the guide was real, Tine could only assume the Guild spied on him. Even now he was unsure just how much privacy he had. One thing he'd learned through observation on Setebos: the more a person claimed something, the less likely it was to be true. There would be no security for him here, despite the locks, the guide, the way they seemed prepared for him.

Which brought him round to his experience in the bistro. After his initial order, various foods had been brought to him, quickly turning to the raw form of his home, all without his asking. At the time he'd been too overwhelmed by the need to eat, and with regret he realized now he'd completely overlooked the fact his requirements had been anticipated. It seemed unlikely that particular bistro had been specifically briefed, and it was beyond the sphere of possibility the staff had simply been familiar with a Caliban's needs.

So, what, then? How had they known? And from where had the Caliban-specific foods come? Somewhere in all those questions lay an answer, he knew. But you also had to know what you were looking for before you could even attempt to find it.

He was interrupted when the air announced Master Ela's arrival. For a moment he considered wiping the screen, but reconsidered. It was quite acceptable for him to have need to record and store information. He was, after all, an Ambassador. Nothing would seem out of place. And if Ela took the time to look at what he analyzed, that might very well play to his advantage.

The air again announced Ela's arrival. Hastily, he trotted across the room and swung open the door. He was as confused as she looked at that moment.

"Is something wrong?" she asked.

Tine went on the alert. "No."

She stepped into the room, brushing past him. "Why didn't you have the auto-systems let me in?" Her gaze darted, resting on the screen.

"Auto-systems?" he asked, deflecting her interest in his activities.

Her attention swung back to him. "You don't have auto-systems on Setebos?"

"No."

"You mean you always physically greet your guests?"

"It's considered a courtesy, and a precaution."

"The precaution I can understand. But a courtesy? Why?"

"A giving of one's time, like saying: You're important enough to infringe on my privacy and so I greet you myself."

She smiled. "Am I?"

Tine's brow wrinkled in a shrug. "Most courtesies become habit. Is it time to go?"

"To go? Oh. Yes. It's time to go." Her glance flicked down to him. "You never wear clothing on Setebos?"

"Calibans don't garb themselves, no. It's not necessary." He made inventory of the elaborate gown she wore, white, a cloud gilded with bursts of light which reminded him of yellow stars. Even the collar which framed her head was like a golden corona. "Why do you?" He was pleased when he saw her confusion.

"I don't know why we garb ourselves," she answered. "I suppose it's like Calibans greeting guests." He winced. She waved to the door. "Shall we go?"

He nodded and trotted out, letting the auto-systems secure the suite. Again he thought of the hut he'd shared with Aganth. Things had been so simple there, uncluttered, given meaning with ritual and the rhythms of the planet. How could he cope with all of this stuff that was Edain?

When they emerged into the ever-present daylight of the street, they were conveyed by floater. By now it came as no surprise, and Tine was secretly pleased he'd adapted so quickly to that mode of transport. To his relief, she made no further attempt at conversation. Up until now communicating with her had been fraught with constant misunderstandings. What he needed to know was evident in everything they passed, in the people, in Ela. Surely something would give him a clue as to what happened to the Gelt Ambassador, even if it was something as simple as the general lack of interest on the part of Edain's natives.

The street on which his hotel was located meandered through a valley of buildings, so that it was easy to become disoriented. Tributaries angled off in every direction, without any apparent organization or planning. Whim seemed the only common factor.

They made a few street changes. Now there were more actual vehicles. Most of these zipped overhead, often leaping buildings. Could it have been that they came from other cities? With such haste? What gave them such haste?

"Just how much of Edain is under domes?" he asked after awhile, risking the confusion of her conversation.

"About forty percent," Ela answered. There was nothing in her tone to encourage him in this area.

That in itself encouraged him. Tine didn't like deflections. And it now seemed curious to him this information had not been made available to him in the brief he'd been presented.

"And the rest?"

"The rest of what?"

"Edain. What is the rest of Edain?"

"Wilderness. I understand Calibans live in the open air."

Ah, deflection. Fine for now. Perhaps at the banquet others would be easier to ply.

"We do," he said. "I'd say our cultures are poles apart. When will I be allowed to address the Guild?" Two could play at deflection.

She glanced sharply at him. "Address the Guild?"

"Yes, address the Guild. That is why I'm here. Setebos would like an envoy from Edain. We could use some guidance in the arts." He felt sure that last statement would open her: Jabod had seemed convinced there was a plot to control governments in the UOoP.

"Forgive me, Ambassador. I've been preoccupied with a tapestry I've been weaving. You're to address the Guild the day after tomorrow."

He nodded, indicating his satisfaction with the latter. He made note of the double-edge of the former. Just what, exactly, had she been weaving?

Weaving? Thread? Tapestry? Warp?

"I'd like an opportunity to see you weave, Master Ela. As a matter of fact, I'd like an opportunity to see as many Masters at their arts as possible."

"I'll see what I can do." She diverted his attention to what at first appeared to be a gargantuan sculpture of an orchid. The artefact dominated a vast plain of green, jade-like material which looked as treacherous as the plaza of amethyst. It wasn't until they drew nearer Tine realized the orchid wasn't a sculpture, rather their intended destination, and, in fact, a building. Things on the throat of the flower moved as though alive. Stem-suckers was the first thought that came to mind, those sweet and sticky insects that clung to vegetation. He swallowed hard when he was able to make out figures in that movement.

"Just how large is this banquet?" he asked, cowed by all this attention. Nothing on Setebos could compare with this scale.

She seemed pleased at having impressed him. "Every Master in the Guild will be there with their mates, concubines, consorts, a few of our more illustrious Adepts—"

"In other words several hundred."

"Several thousand."

He kept his gaze fixed upon the orchid.

Several thousand? From where did all these beings come? Just how large was the population here? Again, the brief he'd been given was vague on these specifics, making reference to a lack of cooperation from Edainian bureaucrats. Using satellite spying had proven ineffective. Conventional infiltration had garnered little. Why hide this information? Why try so hard to impress him? Planetary pride? Hubris? Or was there really something to hide, and thus the obfuscation of fact and information?

His gaze fired around. Passers-by paid less attention to him when he was in Ela's company than when he'd taken his brief jaunt via flying carpet. All of this seemed to be normal to the Edains.

Normal. Perhaps this is all normal pomp to them.

That didn't convince him. He had the feeling he was being set up. For what?

Would it be possible to create an image of me, and have it return to Setebos? Is that what I'm being set up for?

Permanent assignment as his home-world's chief officer seemed suddenly pleasant in its boredom. Right now he'd have been involved in the ritual of random seeding, both the land and his mate. Large harvests and large broods were a sign of wealth. By Caliban standards Tine had been wealthy indeed.

But he'd renounced that. Aganth sealed it with formality. What would she do if he returned, proved to her IPCIB had come up with a way to allow off-planet travel? Would she invoke their vows of union again?

They were descending the orchid's throat before he realized he'd been ignorant of the occurrences of the last few moments. How could he have allowed that to happen? That kind of witless moment, for a successful hunter, could mean death. But, then, he wasn't hunting, was he. Or was he? Wasn't hunting what his role as an IPCIB active on this mission was about? Which thought then brought him to: can my prey turn on me?

He glanced up at Ela, around to the others attending this grand gala, sound crashing round him, gestures, comments, greetings. His moment vanished. Neither predator nor prey. Something else.

"Isn't he beautiful?" one Edainian remarked, audible through the translator uploaded through his conductive nails. The creature had been a quivering lump of clear sepia, all organs—unidentifiable as they were—visible through its mass. He supposed to something like that he would seem beautiful. But to people like Ela, he could be nothing but an oaf. What, then, was beauty? How could one define something so esoteric? And if they weren't able to come to common agreement about matters esoteric, how could they negotiate matters common? Where were the standards, the common ground any of them could find in order to discuss, debate and discover a path of harmony?

He made no response other than to continually nod to Ela's stream of commentary as they continued into the hall, doing his best to acknowledge greetings, fleeting introductions.

When they entered the main cavity of the orchid, it was a universe of light, golden, soft, filled with murmurs. Music drifted on the air. Its melody remained elusive. It was something the body felt rather than heard, and his body was seduced to relax, despite his preoccupation with his mission, the potential for everything to suddenly dissolve and leave him adrift and incapable.

When Ela placed him in a position to receive guests more formally, his discomfort rapidly returned. Faces, or lack of them, went by in a blur. Few of their comments penetrated, mostly inanities of polite society, or so he assumed. It was what they didn't communicate verbally he remembered. It was then he realized he secreted oils, had been rubbing his hide almost continually, cellular memory far more aware of potential jeopardy than his conscious mind. What seemed an eternity later they were seated to table—his set in Caliban fashion, which meant a low platform of pseudo-stone before which he folded his legs and squatted. Again, sights and sensations swept by on a conveyor.

He tasted every assortment of culinary extravagance, all while Ela bent toward him with descriptions of what he savoured. Even for him there was more than he could eat. And beverages, they trickled by in a rainbow of colours, tastes. His mouth tingled with them, his head felt detached, afloat somewhere above. He was sure some of the scents he inhaled were intoxicants.

During all of this, dancers moved with holograms of off-world partners in the bowl of the room; some created their own music in their movements. One of those dancers had been a sentient plant like Tylan. She, or rather it, was astounding. He'd accepted that flora could think, physically react, even move, but he had no idea it could create such an atmosphere of sexuality.

The succulent's fleshy leaves throbbed until the entire arena of the hall pulsed with the sounds of a beating heart, green light adding to the unreality of it. For mammalian life it had been like returning to something primal. Warm. Undeniable. Overwhelming. Every pulse pounded sensation into his skin. The plant's leaves spread, reaching, *I yearn*, vibrating until each participant gasped with pleasure.

Tine's skin crawled, that sensation that told him he was being watched. His gaze shot to Ela. Green light tinted her pale face, her eyes almost luminous, her interest in him evident. Observation? Was that what she'd done throughout this? Observed him? Was the watcher being watched?

It was then he realized there had been little conversation during this spectacle either between himself and Ela, or himself and others. The entire banquet was an orgy of sensations, a gathering where it was impossible to be alone, and yet individuals moved in an utterly isolated universe.

She smiled dreamily. "You've never witnessed the dance of the nepanthaloids?"

He shuddered. "The what?"

"Afra there," she waved to the shrinking creature, "Is one of the nepanthaloid people. You will note how he only made contact with females. He is what we would call male, a descendant from carnivorous beings which inhabited the satellite called Forest. Had he been a primitive, those whom he surrounded would have been dinner. Technology changed that. Nepanthaloids no longer hunt. Now, they surround both their own kind and mammalians to give pleasure—a form of art only they can master."

"You mean he actually—"

"Allowed his guests to orgasm?" She laughed, amused with Tine's incredulity. "Why, of course."

His gaze turned back to the open floor. Afra was now moving back to his place at the assorted and sometimes unidentifiable tables. Tine's gaze flicked over to Tylan. The Master Sculptor quivered slightly. Tine wondered if it were normal, or if the plant-person were reacting to the recent display.

His questions were deflected when an antediluvian humanoid crept into the arena. A noticeable hush fell upon the spectators. Tine suspected the best had been saved for last.

The old man, quite human in appearance, bowed to Tine.

"I, Ambassador Tine, am a dreamweaver." Somehow it signalled danger. He sensed the poised tension in this person, the potential that can only occur when everything hung upon a moment of crisis, fight or flight, predator or prey. "My name, if names are important, is Moishen Ellison, from a homeworld which no longer exists. I, like Master Ela, have been a dreamweaver for as long as I can remember." His glance caught Ela. Moishen's hostility toward her was plain. Tine wondered if Ela saw it, felt it.

Moishen paced to a table and pulled out a chair, placed the chair into the centre of the open floor. "And now," he straddled the chair, his arms folded across the front, "I will spin a yarn."

The lights in the cavernous room dimmed. Tine knew it was to create atmosphere, but the only atmosphere he could feel at the moment was one of tension. There was something subliminal going on here. To pinpoint it was impossible, and yet he was sure the evening was not going according to plan. If his supposition were true, then why wasn't Ela stopping this? Or someone?

The weaver spilled out a pale, yellow light which seemed to generate from his body. His voice was mellifluous, thoroughly controlled and dreamlike. A voice like that could insinuate itself into your subconscious and convince you of anything, cause you to do anything.

"Dreams have always been driving things, things which inflame the minds of mortals, things which shape and reshape standards, things which are the measure by which the dreamer judges her worth.

"Savage, then, was a dreamer—not one who weaves dreams, but one who dreams...."

Tine was mesmerized when Moishen's light seemed

to bulge and then divide. A creature as real as his own flesh moved across the floor. A room appeared around the man, a window showing a stark landscape and a yellow sky with two suns, an easel which held a traditional canvas. A fragrance like tangerines teased Tine's senses, mingling with the resin smells of turpentine, linseed oil, and the chemical bouquets of pigments. A cat-like creature sat in the window, singing, the kind of creature common to Setebos and often domesticated as a pet. The warmth of the breeze indicated the third year of growth called Seihung. It was the day of yellow jasmine, when the plants would bloom and blanket the red soil with woolly perfume. This was to be a day of creativity, in whatever form that creativity took.

The man called Savage made some benign remark to the warbling *yon* in the window. It cooed. He chuckled and turned to the naked canvas. A brush appeared in his hand. Savage began to paint. The canvas grew larger each time his brush stroked the surface. Soon the brush controlled Savage, rather than he controlled the brush. Bloated now, the canvas squatted in the room like an overgrown Caliban. Savage wept, trembling, his face an agony of emotions. The giant Caliban, which had been a canvas, moaned, "Leave me be! Please leave me be!"

Unable to control the brush, Savage's hand quivered when he again touched it to his monstrous creation. Like a tongue, a blue flame waved from Savage's belly. Tine cringed with the creature, *ow, ow, ow it's hot, get it out! Get it out!* Savage's entire torso now erupted in fire, the stink of burning flesh engulfing Tine. The canvas, which was now a Caliban, howled, and then grabbed the painter to his breast, engulfing him in the conflagration. The rest was grizzly, a horror of stinking immolation.

When the carnage ended, only the brush remained.

Moishen's evanescence quieted, drifting off in veils of blue. The only sound was Tine's wailing, wailing which was like the first day of rains when the trees would birth. He became aware that Ela stood over him, medics rushing to his side and that all attention had shifted from Moishen to him. Slowly, he closed his mouth. His throat was a tunnel of heat, molten, coarse.

The message in that story! Why give me a message? They're all supposed to be so dedicated to their art!

He waved off any assistance. His attention returned to the dreamweaver in the bowl of the room who had now arisen and was about to replace the chair. Tine wondered, for a moment, if Moishen were about to mime. The weaver's face became a mask of tragedy. He pitched forward and then sagged over the chair. It seemed burlesque to Tine, the way Moishen's arms were akimbo. Another part of him was screaming, *Look out! Look out! Oh, for pity's sake, look out!* Couldn't they sense the danger here?

Before Tine knew what he did he ran, his hooves clicking against the polished floor, his balance precarious. Urgency kept him upright.

"Get those medics down here!" he roared.

He bent to the weaver, not sure where to check for a pulse on a humanoid.

What was taking those stupid medics so long?

It was then Tine noticed the tiny blue flame darting

from Moishen's belly. Desperate, he threw the weaver onto the floor, and jammed his palms over Moishen's belly, his claws fully distended. The musky odour of his body's oils steadied him. Pain shot through his hands. He roared. Somebody yanked him away. There was a nudge, something bumping up against his brain, his thoughts, something pushing him away. A cloud accumulated over Moishen and then raced for Ela where it disappeared as if she'd swallowed it.

A cloud? Had it been a cloud?

Then there were floaters and more medics, and paths being opened for egress, Moishen's body transported, and in a moment of clarity Tine realized there were others with clear authority who were herding people, casting calm. No one seemed to notice Ela. They should notice Ela. *Look at her,* he thought. She glowed, a corona around her, her face raised toward the ceiling, a look of both ecstasy and fear there, her lips parted. He said her name, heard it lost in the cacophony. Shouts and screams crashed in every direction, the scrape of feet and hooves and other forms of mobility an imperative roar.

Why were they running? What just happened here?

Tine finally noticed the length of his claws. Hastily, he retracted them. His palms tingled where they were burned, and were now healing rapidly.

But I underwent withdrawal. Or at least I thought I underwent withdrawal.

Which made him consider: perhaps Jabod's synthetic wasn't a synthetic. Maybe Calibans had been fed an elegant lie all these years. Keep them backward by denying them off-world travel.

If ideas could go *thunk!* Tine felt sure he'd just heard one drop.

Thread....

His guide had said: *I'm a thread.*

Something else went fell into place.

Dreamweavers weave tapestries. Metaphor carried in related word/ideas: spinning, yarns, weaving, thread, warp, weft....

The guide said: I'm a thread....

Is a thread the weft of a story, the character? And is the character, and a warp, the concept to which that character is bound? Am I, then, a concept?

His claws kept unsheathing, and he struggled to keep that concealed. His anger, however, was not concealed when he turned his gaze up to Ela who now stood as cool and aloof as she had earlier in the day, her moment of transfiguration gone.

"What just happened here?" At the moment he didn't care if any IPCIB authority was betrayed in his manner.

Her answer was calm. "Spontaneous human combustion—one of the hazards of weaving." She inclined her head to the exit. "Shall I escort you to your hotel? I'm sure all of this has been too much for your first day."

TRAVELLING ON the floater beside Ela, he wondered: *What happened back there?* There had been no hunt, no threat, and yet Moishen was transformed to greasy dust. And that cloud. What had that been about? Why did it seem to travel with intent, and why to Ela? Had that been ecstasy on her face? Despair? What was he missing?

And now he felt the fall after the surge, the oils dripping extravagantly over his hide, the imperative to eat, to stuff himself, to replace that burn, so he said, "I need to eat."

That seemed hilarious to him, and he bared his canines in response, turning his face up to Ela.

"Hungry again?" she said, and he watched the way she seemed to gather herself, as though she'd been extended somehow. "Ambassador, you really do consume a great deal." She laughed.

"It's a Caliban thing. We have to." He watched her carefully, aware of the strangeness of her body language, of his own unfamiliarity with things not of Setebos.

He now felt giddy with fatigue, and sleep was something he couldn't yet afford. For a planet that boasted a crimeless society, Ela's response to

Moishen's death had been too calm. She may have called it spontaneous combustion. Everything told Tine that spontaneous Moishen's combustion may have been, but its ignition somehow had to do with Ela. Why else did Ela seem to absorb that cloud which seemed so like a nebula? But he also distinctly remembered Ela warning him, that nudge, and it had been a nudge, something bumping up against his brain, or awareness, or something. The weaver had been trying to warn both him and those whom he addressed. It had been plain to Tine, in retrospect, that the Guild members had been rankled when Moishen walked onto the floor. Something had been out of synch.

Her hand slid across his arm. Contact was brief, but it electrified him. Was he prey? He watched her, trying to find some clue, something that might allow him to know how to respond, but there was nothing. She remained closed. There were no pheromones, no body language, no indicators in her speech; she might have been an artifact for all he could read of her. That was when he asked himself, *Am I safe?*

"Perhaps you should spend the night as my guest," she said. "It's what should have been arranged when we learned there was to be an ambassadorial envoy, and I don't think you should be alone tonight. We can have something to eat there."

Night? The streets were bright with daylight, simulated though it might be. He wondered how Edains kept their sense of time; what was real in a world which dealt with illusion? He looked back at her at that thought, wondering what was real about Ela. *Should I be afraid?*

Again, she laughed, and his claws distended, making a lie of his boast to Jabod.

"If you stay for very long, you'll become accustomed to our cycles."

He realized he'd been given no choice about being her guest. And he also wondered about those arrangements which should, or should not, have been made. Was there a protocol here he should have known about? For the moment he wouldn't object, although all his instincts told him this was an uncertain situation. He felt as though he were assessing a hunt back at home. Was he pursing quarry, or being pursued? Sure he could study the lay of this situation, but when there were no familiar landmarks or signals, it made it nearly impossible to make any kind of assessment. And certainly as he watched Ela, her complete self-possession, her isolation, he wondered just how much Jabod actually knew about her, about what was going on.

He felt as though his guts had just been left behind when their floater angled skyward; he stumbled, sure he'd tumble to the rapidly retreating ground, but he didn't. He saw Ela smile, turn her face away. *Planned? Had that been planned?* If the floater immediately compensated for a user's movements, then why do this to him? Again he asked himself: *am I prey?*

He growled, bared his teeth. She laughed. He was aware his body was reacting as though nothing had changed, as though the spore were still alive and active.

Had Jabod lied? Had all those histrionics of withdrawal been induced?

But why? None of it made any sense. Why set him

up as prey? He had no value as a hostage, could offer no political nor economic advantage.

By now they approached what Tine at first took for a cloud, but in a few moments realized it was some form of ersatz structure. He glanced up at Ela, whose face was set in concentration, an otherwhere look to her as she stared at that mass of constantly shifting, pastel vapour.

Tine realized they were headed into the heart of the thing.

"This is your home?" he asked, surprised at the levelness of his voice.

"Oh, yes," she answered, apparently startled. "Didn't I mention that all Masters live up here?"

"No. Why? Why live up here?"

"For some, isolation is conducive to better creativity. We have no distractions up here."

He wondered about those distractions. And he wondered about all the support industries which weren't evident in any report or survey in his brief. He'd seen evidence enough of artists hawking their wares, from the esoteric to basic needs made weird and wonderful. But then he wondered who was buying those wares? Such an economy depended upon tourism to bring in fresh trade, whether from other bio-domes or off-planet. But that just fed the deeper question of where were the support industries?

Who fed all these people? There was no evidence of industrial scale agriculture, of manufacturing, of any of the systems that maintained the illusion of Edain society. Was all the food, the technology, the material components for their art and their survival brought in from off-planet? And if that were the case, what kind of GDP was Edain producing to pay for all that while still maintaining a quality of life enviable anywhere in the UOoP?

Logically, they required a labour force, whether that pool was comprised of living or manufactured workers, replicators, and technically skilled individuals. And where was that foundation of society when not serving the circus of Edainian life? Where did all the workers live?

An image of Moishen's burning belly hit him. He wondered if that had been the intent of the weaver's tapestry—to warn Edainians about being dominated by the brush of art, rather than dominating the brush. Be an artist or a slave to art. And was that what Moishen had been trying to tell Tine? That there was near revolt here, discontent, an insane society? Was he under threat? Was he prey? Was that the reason Jabod sent Tine to Edain—because he was expendable?

Aganth and her admonition: *You can't run from what you are, Tine.*

The fact he couldn't wasn't as irritating as it had been the day of rebirth. *I am Caliban.* Which meant a great many things. But right now he needed to be the hunter.

He glanced back up at Ela, watched her faint evanescence, like scent hovering around her. She looked down at him, inscrutable, strange. He wasn't sure he could trust her, wasn't sure of how this situation was going to unfold or resolve.

He remembered teaching a litter of his brood how to stalk a Setebian millipede. During the dry years the millipedes were an available food source, but also one which could as easily have you for dinner. He'd fanned out the litter, four females, three males, into pincers around their prey. As they were closing in, the millipede whipped around and sank a barb into hip of the lead female, who roared in fury. He had been sure she would fall right there from the toxins that barb would carry, but she didn't, and he, knowing he battled time as well as this beast, yanked the barb free from his daughter, launched himself onto the millipede's thrashing neck where the quills stopped and the vulnerable temple was exposed, a target not much bigger than his small claw, and drove the quill through that soft membrane and up into the creature's brain. How he stayed his seat while the millipede bucked through its death, he never knew.

In the next moments, he'd kicked in the beast's head, scooped out the gel of its brains and plastered it on his daughter's hip. It was a known cure, if you survived the getting of it.

That night, when they'd tumbled back to their nest, food on their backs, there had been laughter and feasting, stories and songs that spun up into the night with the sparks from the fire.

He knew who he was. And he knew he was in danger.

The entrance to Ela's home was an arch of clouds through which Tine entered an expansive courtyard—mostly a large, rectangular pool, Terran Hellenistic style by his judgement, complete with god-like statues—all surrounded in the ubiquitous pastel clouds that made up Ela's environment. The entire effect was tranquil, a study of reflections and light.

He observed none of it had any affect upon Ela, who made no pause nor comment, and led him through another arch of cloud into a small space. It was then Tine realized even the walls were made of this nebulous, intangible stuff so that he lost his sense of space and time. He wasn't even sure where his hooves were.

Her home seemed to go on forever. He wondered how he'd find his way around. Being in his hotel had been bad enough. This might prove insurmountable. Here, there seemed to be no other inhabitants than Ela; it was, as she said, complete isolation.

At length, after guiding him through several spaces and corridors—for what did she need all this space—she led him into a chamber which was bright, warm, and to Tine's delight, assembled in the fashion of a Caliban ritual eating area. He was salivating noticeably when she waved him to his ease, which he did with care, always watching, unsure, aware an escape might prove difficult.

She asked as she lowered herself into the clouds, "On what would you care to dine, Ambassador?"

"Something substantial."

Her brow arched, but without any comment from her, leaves and treen filled with food from Setebos appeared on the stone table, cages with live specimens. He ate quickly. Ela kept from distracting him with conversation, and that proved to be a distraction. By the time he'd slurped his last mouthful, he was again holding Ela's intentions suspect.

Finally, she said, "You've told me very little about your culture, Ambassador. It would be interesting to hear some of your customs."

He had the feeling her point of interest was centered in an area she preferred to address obliquely.

He managed what he felt was a facsimile of a smile, sure he was not equipped to enter into this discussion. For a moment he ruminated on words, cast this phrase aside, that statement, and then: "We are simple by comparison to you, Master Ela."

"Simple?"

"We deal with ritual, structure, tradition—"

"Bondage."

"Yes. To the planet."

"But apparently no longer."

Apparently? "Yes. Apparently."

"You say that almost with regret."

He remembered nights on Setebos, the import of them, the seeming power of ritual. The rite of the moons when gravity pulled the planet into a flurry of growths. History made living through their shared stories, traditions and laws, the parables of a people tested and shaped by an environment they both loathed and loved.

Did he regret that all of what he knew was now open to the rest of the UOoP? Would Setebos change? Would his people be able to find their way through the flood of what was to come?

Would there be domes? Would those who immigrated want to deny the night as they did on Edain? It was then he confronted the fact that to deny the wild power within each of them was to deny what you were.

Did he regret the lifting of his planet's quarantine?

"Yes," he said at length. "There is regret."

"Why? Edain and the rest of the UOoP could offer you so much."

"As if we're in need of so much."

"Aren't you?"

"We have shelter. We have food. We have the surety of our broods."

"Don't you find that restrictive?"

He remembered thinking exactly that just recently. He'd been so eager to go, to leave, to explore, and throw himself into the feast of what awaited him away from Setebos. Free of responsibility. Free of bondage.

You can't run from what you are, Tine.

"Not until recently. Isolation can keep out as well as keep in."

Adroitly, he caught the way her nostrils flared. He'd achieved some form of reaction, slight as it may have been. A reaction to what? Why?

"Then why the need for an Edain envoy?" she asked.

"Our planet is opening. We'll no longer be bound by spore symbiosis, which can now be manufactured synthetically." At least that's what he'd been told. "Because of that, one of Setebos' first priorities is to invite artists to study our culture, and so we may study theirs, and through that exchange gain understanding. What better way to do that than to have representatives of the Guild interact with us?

"The liaison should prove fruitful. You'll be allowed a new pool of recruits for Edain, and we'll be able to update and broaden our knowledge. Simple economic sense."

"But won't our people be affected by the spore? I understand incompatibility proves lethal."

"As I have said, the new synthetic negates all that." Even as he said it he had doubt. The reports and Jabod's interaction were now suspect.

"Will it be like spore symbiosis?"

"It will have to be. There are few compromises with Setebos."

Her fingers brushed her bare arm. "What will that do to a subject?"

He glanced at her fingers, back up to her face. He shuddered with unexpected pleasure. "The spore produces high levels of alpha-tocopheryl acetate, simply known as vitamin E, which will allow adaptability to variable oxygen levels, as the body then requires less oxygen in blood tissues. There will be other side effects."

"Such as?"

What is she driving at?

"Development of a thick epidermis. I don't know if an alien would develop a Caliban's pockets—"

"Pockets?"

He watched her gaze dart over his body, felt freakish under her scrutiny, and suddenly he was back home, with Aganth and his brood, surrounded by familiar faces and familiar days. When Ela raised her brows in question, he pressed one of the warts on his chest, allowing it to gape open into a purple hole. He winced at her expression, closing the pocket.

"They're extremely sensitive," he said, "erogenous. That's another thing about the spores—they form a protective, insulating barrier that nourishes cellular ability to burn fats, hence our—what you would call—large, frequent appetites. As a by-product, adrenaline is in rapid, ready supply. We heal almost instantaneously, have a high tolerance to pain, and a driving need to procreate. Excitement usually stimulates both adrenal glands and sex hormones. I would assume the same symptoms will occur in aliens who undergo symbiosis. But I don't know; this is only what I've been told."

She nodded, apparently satisfied, rose and gestured to a door beyond. Her smile was coy as she led him from one room to another. He followed, tingling with alarm. There would be a fight or flight situation here. He was sure of it.

As bright as the previous room had been, so was this room equally dark. Tine felt as though darkness sucked upon his flesh—ugliness mating with ugliness. This was so foreign to what he knew about darkness, about the laughter and ease there had been in the surety of a strong brood and strong, bonded couple. There had been starscapes, moonscapes, firelight to define the night. Never had he known such complete, consuming darkness. This darkness—Ela's darkness—crept over him like secrets and oblivion, a void that drank light and swallowed life. And in that void, there was Ela, evanescent, strange, and terrible.

He watched her, that aloofness, that amusement, as though she were tolerating not only him but everyone he had seen her encounter. Ela functioned from a perspective different from her peers. That had been obvious when he first met her, and remained obvious now.

Why bring him here?

He realized he was rubbing oil into his hide, that he was exuding prodigiously. He looked back up. There in the darkness Ela's face shone with a pale, golden radiance that made him think of ancient stars in final glory. It was then he realized he'd been able to note the expression on her face because of its luminosity, but what her face revealed was difficult to interpret. Amusement, definitely. Coyness? Perhaps. Aroused or merely curious? A hunter assessing her prey? Very likely.

Light played over his hide, pressure in its presence, pleasure in its touch. His heart kicked. He started to back away, seeking flight, heard her voice: *Don't,* and touched his aural warts, wondering where the sound had come from, because her lips never moved. He felt the wart concealing his sex stiffening, distending, tenting with unspeakable urgency so that he knew he would have to find a way to unsheathe his penis from its protective glove or suffer from severe agitation that might end in violence.

Why is she doing this?

There, in that heinous darkness, he wanted to impale Ela with his need. The scent of his own sexuality was like fire in his nostrils.

Corruption! What's happening?

Just out of arm's reach she kept smiling that haughty, distant smile. The golden glow of her face crept down to her neck, her bare shoulders, and then illuminated the cloth of her gown. The garment seemed to dissolve under his stare. Warm, seductive light slipped over her tiny breasts, her waist, girdled her thighs until she shone completely.

Realization! Dreamweavers usually glowed when

they were spinning. But Ela wasn't spinning. She just kept staring at him with that detached amusement.

He was so engrossed in her effulgence he hadn't noticed anything else. Now there were hands, warm and demanding travelling the sheath of his sex. Desperate, he tried to keep himself from exposing. He shuddered. Too late.

Ela still stared at him, predominant now, almost as if she willed him to look into her eyes while those hands shoved him beyond restraint.

"Don't do this to me, Ela," he groaned. There hadn't even been any ritual between them as there had between he and Aganth, a slow circling of each other, an opening and closing of pockets, a haunting kind of clicking-humming which would accent their actions.

Ela didn't reply verbally. Her thumb and forefinger pinched the nipple of her left breast. Tine's mouth watered with want. His tongue flicked over his lipless mouth. In the next moment he found his teeth brushing against another breast, the nipple like silk in his mouth. With a moan he sucked deeply, still held by Ela's gaze.

Even as he realized that, he knew, without seeing, that another man slowly, agonizingly slowly, parted those hot inner recesses between Ela's thighs—thighs for which Tine ached.

All thought of her alienness fled. Tine didn't care if she wasn't Caliban, if her blood were some vague other colour than crimson. He wanted to spill his own seed inside her, to feel her almost non-existent breasts press against his chest, to have the sweaty warmth of her thighs wrap tightly around his back.

As Tine peered around, he saw the shadow of a man beneath the woman who pleasured his sex. From there the scene was grotesque. There were every species of sentient life in the room, some with several orifices, others clearly hermaphrodites, a few with multiple hands. The throb of a nepanthaloid syncopated their movements.

Horrified, he drowned in the demands of the orgy. His urgency broke the bonds of restraint. Somehow he managed to claw his way to Ela who was still smiling. He didn't even bother to taste her lips, lips which were wide and fleshy and so alien to the puckered Caliban O of flesh. No ritual. His mouth claimed her nipples. Something vaguely like bitter honey gushed over his tongue. His head swam. And then he sank his penis into a tunnel of excruciating heat. His breath was ragged. Blind panic swept over him as his passion swelled. He felt as though Ela robbed him of the essence of his life, sucking it all through this act of sex. But he couldn't deny her. This wild desire knew no bounds. It demanded that he take her alien flesh. And so he knew he was bound to her, physically unable to withdraw from her until the act was complete.

And then the tip of his penis burned as it fountained sperm into her body. He felt as though she yanked blood, veins, arteries, organs, brain—all through his sex.

He screamed. He fell away.

Tine retched, oblivious of any onlooker who might find him, desperate to purge himself of the vile thing he'd known. His ears filled with the sound of Aganth's humming, the tune she breathed in the warmth of afterglow. None of this would be his now.

When his heaving was no more than dry, shuddering coughs, he backed away and huddled into a dark corner, a beast trapped by what he was, duped, manipulated, and used.

The figures dissolved into the air. Ela's radiance paled. There was still that haughty look on her face. He could barely meet her gaze.

"So now you've had a dreamweaver," she said. "How does it feel, Caliban?"

He flinched. She reminded him of his ugliness. Everything from Setebos was ugly.

*We are what our environment makes us. There
is no escape and no exception.*
                    IPCIB Operations Manual

THIS WAS a game Ela never enjoyed—that of political subterfuge. She enjoyed it even less now she was with Master Tylan, the Master Sculptor, although she would play her part with precision. When it came to her purpose, she could allow no deviation. It was necessary for the Guild to believe they needed her, that she was integral to their plans of takeover in the UOoP and IPCIB. Fulfill that role and her real purpose would be served—she hoped. So much depended on Tine, on convincing him that dreamweavers were entities no one in the UOoP had ever known.

She turned back to the giant aloe, watching the way Tylan vibrated to the impulses from the other plants in this jungle he called home. Such a curiosity. She remembered the orchid she'd woven for him, right here, on this very spot, the way he'd been captivated by her tapestry, convinced it was real. It had been at that moment she realized her dual purpose with him would succeed. Even now she was convinced, despite recent problems.

The aloe spasmed. A voice followed the movement, a voice which issued from no orifice. "That was a foolish mistake you made with the Gelt Ambassador."

She kept her demeanour cool, as if nothing Tylan would do could touch her. "Considering the enormity of the ruse I've woven for IPCIB and the UOoP, my error with the Gelt Ambassador was minimal."

"But the thread you wove of him dissolved. They'll suspect murder."

"And we're suspect? I think not."

"Don't be a fool, Ela! Edain was the last place the Gelt was seen alive."

"That does nothing to implicate the Edain Guild." She laughed. "You really are far too paranoid, Tylan."

"Paranoid or not, I don't want this to happen again."

"I assure you it won't."

"Your assurances do little to comfort me. The entire Guild has seen already that you're not infallible."

She shrugged. "Then let someone else weave your tapestry of falsehoods and subterfuge."

"You're in this just like the rest of us."

"I didn't say I wasn't. But it would be wise to constrain your criticisms. Without me the Guild's entire plan falls."

Tylan trembled in his pot, his long, fleshy leaves vibrating like green swords. "I'm all too aware of how much we need you."

They did need her. That was the beauty of it. They needed her to weave threads, to weave characters to replace the people the Guild wanted to control. It was Ela who convinced the Guild that bribery of officials in the UOoP and IPCIB wasn't enough. Bribery led to avarice or sudden seizures of conscience. By replacing these key officials with characters she wove it guaranteed they would act precisely as she wished.

And that served her ultimate purpose. While the Guild thought the officials she replaced had been conveniently killed, she had, in fact, spirited them away to a place in the undomed regions of Edain where they were held by other dreamweavers, what the Guild kept thinking of as rebels. The most recent hostage had been the IPCIB Commissioner, Jabod McCullough. All she needed now was Tine.

Tylan's house security chimed. He answered. It informed him of the Setebos Ambassador's presence. He grunted permission to enter, trembling, writhing as if trying to break free of the pot binding him.

"What do you mean you left him alone?" he barked, letting the electronic interpretation of his anger hit her.

Ela smiled. "He has no suspicion of our problems. Everything's fine, Tylan. If he doesn't know for what to look, how can he look?"

"You assume too much, Ela! The rebels take advantage of every opportunity possible. Do you think it wise to risk the Ambassador's enlightenment?"

The rebels. What would happen if Tylan finally realized it was the dreamweavers the Guild should fear most? What would happen if he realized she was the head of this rebellion?

"The rebels won't concern our Caliban visitor," she said. "I guarantee that." Lies could be so easy to tell. It was just another form of storytelling.

"How can you guarantee that when the rebels constantly disrupt what goes on in the work-warrens?"

For a moment, she almost shouted at him in anger,

condemning him for the crime of the work-warrens. To use children in the work-warrens was bad enough, but to use dreamweaver children was worse. He had no idea what danger waited to explode around them.

"Just because of that," she answered. "The rebels are more interested in what goes on in the work-warrens than from some visiting dignitary."

But that, she knew, was also a lie. The rebels were very much interested in this visiting dignitary, in this Caliban Ambassador. Everything she'd discovered about Setebos indicated Tine would understand the dreamweavers better than anyone in the Guild. He'd survived her dark tapestry, that initial test. Tine was her only hope.

Echo the walls. Echo the walls with sound. Echo the walls with the sounds of home so that joy is the vibration to which you move.

CALIBAN SONG.

HE WANTED to excise the memory of that orgy, cut it out like a diseased organ, divorce it in the way Aganth divorced him and wiped record of his existence from their family. For the first time, he understood a little of how she might have felt: violated, betrayed.

How could he have succumbed? He felt as though he'd balanced on the edge of a precipice and wilfully stepped into the void, a place from which he could never return. How was he to navigate his way from here? How to find the path that would lead him to redemption in the eyes of his brood? What was more, how to give himself that gift, because as much as he detested the reality, he realized his destiny was entirely of his own making. He was responsible for Aganth's hurt. He was responsible for his separation from kith and kin. And in the end only he was responsible for the darkness of that night. His. His responsibility.

He lay on his back, upon a bed of clouds, humiliation a stone in his gut.

He barked a command to the unseen controls. Darkness swallowed the area. He found comfort in its concealment. But it wasn't long before he realized he longed for concealment from himself, not his surroundings. Darkness reminded him of that room. Such horror there. He'd participated with a nauseating sense of fascination, incapable of doing anything to prevent his humiliation. It had all been so unreal, so dreamlike. More nightmare, were he honest.

What happened to me? he wondered. *Was it even real?*

The fact he questioned reality set all his senses on alert, and in response he rubbed the oils from his warts into his hide, all the while rubbing a question he'd asked himself over and over again: *What's real in a world filled with illusion?*

The question remained unanswered. He still turned that thought when he woke, abruptly and with fear.

His room was again radiant with light. He could only assume Ela made a change in his command. She'd checked on him. Why? What could she possibly want with him now he was so utterly humiliated? But then maybe he afforded himself greater notice than warranted. What evidence did he have Ela observed him? Maybe the lights were set on an automatic function.

You think too much. And in thinking that he heard Aganth chiding him over some IPCIB report with which he'd been wrestling. *All you do is look for connections. Did it ever occur to you that sometimes things are simply random? That connections only exist because of your obsession?*

But it was his obsession that made him valuable to IPCIB. Bound as he'd been to Setebos, he was still able to be one of Jabod's top analysts.

Hunger ravaged his stomach. He swung his legs over the edge of the cloud and dangled his hooves into vapour, watching eddies swirl out across the horizontal plane that was the floor, sweep up the vertical of a wall and curl down and drift into the space of the room.

"Is Master Ela here?" he asked the clouds.

A disembodied voice answered, "Master Ela is at Council. She will return at twelve."

"And the time now?"

"Four."

"Ah-h." He nodded. Eight units of time to fill until he could table his questions to her. "Bring me food, the same in quantity as I was fed last night."

"As you wish, Ambassador. It will be served in the dining area."

"I don't know where that is."

"Follow the rooms to your right."

He slid off the cloud, burying his legs to the knees in vapour. There was a water closet adjoining his room, and after making use of it, he trotted off in the direction the house system indicated. The entire construct of Ela's house was one of illusion, chamber after chamber without seeming function or purpose, like a warren of caves scooped out of mist. The dining area, as the house indicated, was found by constantly heading to the right, and once there he found a low table of vapour laden with an assortment of vegetables, fruits and small, caged animals. He ate perfunctorily, with haste and discomfort.

By the time he was done, he'd selected a course of action, sketched a keyboard into the vapour of the table and stabbed out a text message to Jabod: *Send in a sonic sweep, my coordinates, URGENT.* His demand was acknowledged, cleared, sealed under a security lock known only to IPCIB. He turned away as Jabod's message flashed across his retina.

It would be prudent for him to be absent when the sweep arrived. He might even manage to rendezvous with Ela and give the technician a margin of safety.

When he trotted out of the room, he asked, "Am I going the right way for exit, and can I get a floater when there?"

"Yes to both, Ambassador. Where shall I say you have gone?"

"To an understanding." He left the walls inquiring after him as he sped away into the sky.

From this height the biodome was even more bizarre. There was no main centre, no environmental sympathy. The entire city was a construct of whim. Where were the urban planners, the authorities that laid out a metropolis in a fashion that allowed business and residence to coexist? Not a problem on Setebos where the cultural demands were different, but here? This was a dense, highly organized society, removed from natural environment. Again Tine wondered at the lack of business. Services there were in abundance. But beyond that the machinery that underpinned this society was absent. He wondered if Moishen, the dreamweaver who had combusted, had known how profound his tapestry had been, how insightful.

Of course he had, Tine thought. Moishen's had been a cry of protest snuffed before it could gain momentum. Or had it? There were agendas here, plans within plans, and Tine but a pawn, he realized, put into play by IPCIB, played by The Guild, pushed by Ela. When did the puppet cut the strings? When did the puppet realize it could walk on its own?

Now, Tine thought. I can do this now. Whatever *this* is.

He inhaled sharply, feeling the breeze of his passage cool on his skin. His gaze shifted to where the dome curved. In a ring near the perimeter floated the other homes of the Guild, each as eldritch as the next; below them were the city portals connecting Edain's other urban centres with the capital. Tine thought of a web.

What do they catch in their web? he thought. What exactly had Moishen been trying to say? Had it been as Tine earlier suspected, a direct message from Moishen to him? Was Tine the prey in the web?

Traffic in and out of these links was constant, although not voluminous, every manner of conveyance imaginable, all improbable, all illusion he was sure. There were carpet riders and beasts pulling carriages made of every conceivable material, from overgrown squash to golden spheres. Palanquins were trotted along avenues. People glided on unseen vapour. Winged creatures, swimming, galloping, slithering—it was like watching dreams on parade. And still he could see no evidence of any industry other than the arts. How to generate the power required for all these illusions that affected reality, that made a lie of gravity, and bent the laws of physics? Were these power generators beyond the domes, hidden from the aesthetics of Edain's ruling class? And if industry lay beyond the domes, how to

Caliban

populate those areas when the undomed regions were allegedly dangerous to most life forms? Was there a life form that could survive out there? As with all other information he'd received about Edain, details regarding the wilderness beyond the domes had been vague. Had that been a result of lack of research, or lack of cooperation? Why was the Guild withholding information?

Master Tylan's home was now in view—at least, what Tine assumed was the sculptor's home. As he drew nearer, he was able to give definition to the dark island. It was indeed like an island, crowned in rain forest which was lush, and dense, and brilliantly green. Tine couldn't remember ever seeing such an expanse of verdancy, and the closer he came the smaller he felt, overshadowed by a forest unlike anything he'd ever known on Setebos, and unlike anything he'd researched. The only thing to which he could compare this was the towering cathedral of ancient Earth forests, where the sky was blotted from view by a canopy impossibly high, and trees spanned millennia rather than centuries.

His insignificance was tangible when the floater deposited him at a hole in the forest. Birds trilled through the gloom. Humidity clung to his skin, the musky scent of forest duff heavy. A cry overhead brought his gaze up, just in time to catch the swinging figure of some form of lemur. The auburn mass of fur had eyes as yellow as his own. Tine grinned. The creature shrieked at him and rained fruits down on his head. He was about to bend down to inspect one of the red globes when two serpents slid around his ankles.

A hollow voice demanded, "What business have you here?"

He was again shocked by the Edain sense of security. What was so hostile that they'd interrogate every visitor?

Tine growled at the serpents and they disengaged. He stamped his hooves.

"Requesting an audience with Master Tylan. Tell him it's the Setebian Ambassador."

"Enter, Ambassador. Follow the yellow bird to Master Tylan's studio."

His escort popped into view, twittering and fluttering in a frenzy. Just as had been indicated, the bird displayed a direction. Seemed there was nothing for it but to follow the thing.

As intangible as was Ela's home, so was Tylan's tangible, despite the fact Tine knew it, like all else here, was an illusion. It reminded him of the days of growth on Setebos, when the fruit trees exploded from the earth and screamed as they reached maturity. That was the closest he'd ever come to walking through a forest.

The bird, winking like sunlight through trees, led him on a meandering course which took them over streams, fallen trees, fronds of ferns. Flowers bloomed profusely from the odorous floor to the canopy. Here he could lose his sense of purpose. This had the demand of reality.

Presently he heard voices, no distinguishable words, but the definite rhythm of conversation. It rose and fell like the susurration of waves. And then: "What do you mean you left him alone?" Harsh words. Anger. They broke the delicate rhythm.

There was something odd about that voice, something almost mechanical, menacing.

Another answered, "He has no suspicion of our problems. Everything is fine, Tylan. If he doesn't know for what to look how can he look?"

Tine froze, tensing. He rubbed at his chest, smoothing oil into his skin.

That was Ela!

He shuddered.

At council with Tylan...normal enough...but why did he get the feeling nothing was normal?

"You assume too much, Ela!" That was the first speaker. Tine assumed it was Tylan. Why was he so angry? "The rebels make advantage of every opportunity possible. Do you think it wise to risk the Ambassador's enlightenment?"

His enlightenment? So, there was something they wished to hide from him. Rebels?

For a moment, he deliberated whether to leave or take his audience. The latter, upon consideration, seemed wiser. He could at least pose his questions, and the answers, whether verbal or implied, would give him an indication of what to do next.

The argument stalemated, much of it lost in the forest's chatter. When Tine stepped into Tylan's studio—a clearing in the trees—Ela simmered with an emotion he couldn't cipher. It was as though this woman, the master of Masters, was accusing the sentient plant of some crime. He glanced from one to the other for a moment, trying to find his bearings, reading nuances, and it was then he realized he was using his hunter instincts, and that was a surprise and a revelation in itself. It was in that moment he realized Ela had none of these primal talents at her disposal. Hers was a world of illusion and intellect. Tine very much had the feeling Tylan knew all about survival methods. A species of sentient plants didn't evolve by being passive. In that moment Tine pitied Ela. Whatever her role, whatever her alliance, she would be thwarted by those capable of reading and responding to the elemental.

That revelation unfolded another. Pity was a new understanding. On Setebos there was no room for pity. One adapted. One survived. Life fitted an order and a balance in the natural scope of the universe. To pity was to give way to sentiment and sentiment could lead to death.

He stepped completely into the light of the clearing. His feathered escort twittered and popped out of existence. The giant aloe spasmed. A voice followed that movement.

"Welcome, Ambassador Tine."

Tine looked over at the nepanthaloid, unsure how to proceed, unsettled by the interpreter to which the creature was connected. "Master Tylan?"

"Yes, Ambassador. You requested an audience?"

He caught the flicker of strong emotion on Ela's face.

"I did...yes...Master Tylan...."

Ela laughed. "Tylan, my dear, our Ambassador is unfamiliar with your species. You might be a little more diplomatic and explain how you function." Her smile was beguiling when she swept toward Tine, her touch as light and brief as the brush of a butterfly. "Be at ease, Ambassador. Tylan seeks pleasure in the discomfort of others, and now you have caused discomfort in him. Not a situation he enjoys. He has told me that a form like yours demands attention by the arts, and he is insistent a likeness of you will be his next coup de grace at next year's exhibition. Be a pet and soothe his ugly temper." She nodded to both of them, turned and seemingly floated from the room, calling over shoulder, "I'll expect you for dinner, Ambassador."

Tine watched as she left, wondering why Ela hadn't attempted the stage. Incapable she might be of dealing with primitive situations, but in a game of diplomacy she was formidable. Again, he turned to the nepanthaloid sculptor.

"My apologies, Master Tylan," he began, electing bumpkin diplomacy. Perhaps by displaying his non-comprehension of Edain it might tempt this unknown quantity to enlighten him. "I didn't mean to interrupt a moment of creativity."

As before, the aloe pulsed. It was only a slight movement, almost invisible, but enough that Tine caught it. As he expected, a voice issued from the pot area.

"No interruption, Ambassador. Please. Make yourself comfortable."

Tylan's pot pivoted on what Tine assumed were lifts.

He wondered what was front and what was back to the spiky creature, or for that matter, how Tylan visualized, if at all. Was Tylan's world transmitted through sensory input outside of conventional vision? Did he visualize in the ultra-violet band? Or beyond?

Tine did as he was bidden—made himself comfortable—and squatted as he would have in his home.

"At least we're even," he said at length, watching as a chunk of wood lifted toward the sculptor. "You're as strange and new to me as I am to you."

"Indeed. Then I suggest we trade question for question to keep the scales of enlightenment in balance."

Balance. Everything would have to be balanced with Tylan, vulnerability for vulnerability.

"Fair.... How do you speak?" Tine asked, taking the advantage of first knowledge.

The block of wood Tylan had selected shed chips like a shower of feathers, without use of any tool.

"All life generates energy," Tylan answered, his voice nasal, mechanical. "Energy can be channelled into language. Between nepanthaloids, these shifts in energy impulses can be monitored through air pressure. It's partly in this manner we communicate. We also release pheromones. Each combination says something different, much in the way you would construct a sentence. In order for us to communicate with species such as yours, we're fitted with translators which are embedded in our pots—"

"So that's not your real voice?"

"Unfair, Ambassador. That's two questions. It's my turn."

Tine grimaced. "You're right."

"Why are you here?"

"To address the Guild with a petition from Setebos. You know that."

"And that petition?"

"Ah-ah-ah, Master Tylan. My turn."

The thing the sculptor was creating began to take shape, although what shape that was Tine was unsure. The point of his curiosity was stuck on the mechanics of how Tylan sculpted, not what.

"What about industry?"

"Art is our industry."

Tine simmered on that. Why hide their industry?

"Your petition?" Tylan asked. "What might that petition be, exactly."

Single-minded, Tine thought. Tylan had scented his prey and was on the hunt. "Setebos would like to have an Edain envoy." He tried a different tack on his former question. "Where's your industry that is unrelated to art?"

"I can't think of any industry that isn't artful. What makes you think Edain would consider your proposal?"

"We're the only planet without an envoy. I'm sure you'd like to enlighten back-planet bumpkins. So... where do your rebels hide?"

Tine held his breath, waiting for something explosive to happen. There was no answer for several minutes, and then, surprisingly, the sculptor said calmly, "We have no rebels, Ambassador. I'm afraid you're misinformed." Tine could almost hear the smile in Tylan's voice. "We've had no crimes here."

"I see your point, Master Tylan. It's difficult to have crime when there are no laws."

The chips fell in a sheet.

That hit home!

He bowed. "Thank you for the audience, Master Tylan. Oh, a little advice: Next time you're going to sculpt me, ask for permission. Calibans have been known to kill over lesser breaches of privacy."

Tylan was screeching when Tine trotted away.

In order for you to sit in enlightened judgement on this jury, it is necessary for you to understand just what, exactly, a dreamweaver is, and what a dreamweaver does. I do not attempt interpretation of the following excerpt from an IPCIB sonic sweep of Master Ela's home. Rather, I simply accept the facts as they are presented. That is something you must do—accept facts.

What has evolved on Edain is something beyond imagination. Only if you accept these facts on instinct can you decide if the Edain Guild is innocent or guilty of slavery.

THE EDAIN TRIAL, JURY ADDRESS
DREAMWEAVER COMMISSIONER TINE

IF **IS** such an enormous word. It encompasses infinite possibilities. *If* I do this. *If* I am successful. *If* I fail. *If* hopes and dreams are realized. *If* hope and dreams die. *If* I die.

When I die.

If disappears. At least from my reality.

And so the story goes. The story, the yarn, the tapestry, the weaving of a life. There was one culture that spoke of the Moirai, the three sisters Clotho, Lachesis and Atropos, busily spinning out the lives of mere mortals. That myth is to be found in many cultures. It is notably absent from Setebos, the home planet of my major *If,* the Ambassador Tine.

If his culture does not embrace the concept of fate, of realities controlled by another sentience, then it might follow he will have a very firm grasp of reality. But then perhaps not. It would seem Calibans—and Tine seems no exception—embrace the transient and illusory nature of existence. That may work both for and against my task, one not dissimilar to that triumvirate of sisters, those ladies of warp and weft and weavers of destiny.

And now I have to ask myself if—that word again—I have not become one of that trinity, whether spinner of life's story, apportioner of life's length, or the implacable sister who will not be turned from the task of destiny. Regardless, I am myth. I and my kind. Dreamweavers. Spinners of stories. Makers of realities.

The tragedy of it is *if* I cannot make my reality known, *if* I cannot prove the existence of something for eons thought merely dreams, then dreams cease, *if* no longer a possibility, *if*—the great optimism of every living, sentient thing. If.

If I spin. *If* I weave. *If* spinning seizes me, the imperative of that nebulous *if,* for there is a question *if* I will succumb to the reality of what I am, that I will do what nature has made me to do. I am a dreamweaver, born that way, although to say I was born implies flesh and blood and a dramatic mess of fluids and wails. Depending on the reality, it can also mean a silent screaming stretching through darkness toward light, and forever after in competition for that light. Life, a bursting forth. Whatever life means.

But for a dreamweaver, those of us who are created in the Skeins, in the undomed regions of Edain, we have no memory of struggle, of the tearing of flesh, of the race for light. We do not remember parentage, home—matters of import to others. What we do remember is our origins. And that has nothing to do with parentage. We were this mass, and then another, an atom and then a molecule and then a multitude, so that when we are legion we then weave, create, incarnate realities.

These things are the mark of a dreamweaver. They are the mark of a species unknown to the others of this universe. They are part of the dreamweavers who do all the tasks of distaste for the Edains.

We, that is dreamweavers, find ourselves confused by this preoccupation of others with doing. The doing seems to be important. But for us, we simply are. That which the Guild calls doing, we are. I cannot make them understand that only we are dreamweavers. They do not understand what we are. We are not in their reality. For them we don't exist. To them we are gifted writers without peer. We create realities, stories if you will—tapestries we call them.

I am avoiding this task before me. It is necessary for dreamweavers to make themselves known. Time is of essence. These others, these aliens, cannot continue to live and expand on our native planet. Dreamweavers, we have found, are incompatible with their forms of life. We are a danger to them. As I exist, I'm not a threat, as neither are others like me who live in the domes of Edain. Our masses haven't accumulated to the point we can each exist in our own looms—our own territories.

I came into this room—such a lovely, lightless room—to weave. It reminds me of nights in the Skeins. Nights when dreamweavers compress, causing incandescence as hydrogen is burned away from our envelopes, and in the burning create our own realities, worlds, and people we suppose we might become in some other reality. We imagine. We make if. And therefore we create. And therefore we are. Of course to create also means we can uncreate, which is quite different from the ability to create and then destroy. We make reality. We unmake reality. Until now that hasn't been a problem.

The problem now is that other realities, not of our own making, enter our realities, become part of our dreams, and when you share a dream that reality becomes embedded in another life form, and so the undoing, the unmaking, causes distress to the unsuspecting life form. It doesn't comprehend, as we do, that reality is relative, that substance, shape, and form are given life because an individual chooses to believe that thing, that reality, exists.

I find myself asking, what is real in a world where reality can be made and unmade?

It is because I've asked that question, that very flesh and blood question, that my fellow dreamweavers have convinced me that I and only I can realize any hope of success in making our reality known to these others who have claimed Edain as their own. I feel like someone shouting from the wilderness, "Hello! Hello! We're here, hello!" And there is no response. I do not exist. Or the method of communication has no common ground. Or. If. What if?

Dimensions.   Realities.   Universes.   So   many

possibilities creating distances between us. And no easy bridge between. I walk on space. It is so easy. And watch the people of Edain fall as they try to follow.

The spell of weaving is upon me again. It's demanding. There's no escape from the need to weave—just like their need to sleep, eat, breed. Without weaving I am impotent and without identity, my mass divided among the others, and that, in itself, is a danger. One weaver with too great a mass, while weaving, could surge and that could consume this single-planet system.

So I must weave tonight. Soon the images will wind in my mind like ghosts of places I have been, or have yet to be, or yet to make.

I wait.

Why won't the images come? I need to weave! Without the images the tapestry won't unfold. It doesn't matter if the tapestry isn't completed now, this moment, but I must weave! Now! Before I escort Ambassador Tine to the work-warrens. I must be in a stable state then. I must make him aware of our existence and of our plight.

There are so many warps in my head which demand weaving: the Wart on the rug I've given to Tine for his own protection, four Actives within the Bureau, eight in the Gelt Consortium, including the Gelt Ambassador's thread I created to set a snare....

I can't remember the others. Why can't I remember? I must remember all the threads for this tapestry to complete itself. Without this tapestry, I will be unable to make others aware of our reality: that dreamweavers exist as something other than what they understand.

Where are the sisters of this trinity I have become?

I need to weave. The other threads aren't creating a tapestry that enables me to express my reality. They are simply warps with a difficult destiny. A tapestry requires not only warp, but weft, pattern, a reason to unfold into a particular texture and pattern which inevitably reflects on the weaver.

Let the darkness blanket you. There are no distractions here, no demands made by the Guild. For this moment, you can be Ela the dreamweaver, as you were first in the Skeins, not Ela the Master Dreamweaver of the Edain Guild.

The Guild.

They look to me because I am the only one capable of making their realities come true. They want to control the governments of their parent solar system to ensure the prosperity of the arts and social commentary. I live in their reality also, and for them I weave.

How I weave.

I remember a time I wove so well I created a lover for our dear Tylan—Tylan the sentient plant. Tylan the Master Sculptor. Tylan who snatches light and bends it in ways that makes it tantalizingly real. Tylan who is a threat, I'm sure.

She was an orchid—his lover. Oh, yes, she had to be exotic, something reminiscent of all I understand to be female, something which would make Tylan's instincts flower. And he did! Tylan actually flowered for my orchid.

How strange it was to feel him woo and fertilize her. How very strange. It will prove to be interesting research for a future tapestry.

But now I'm caught in a political arena in which I must weave never-ending stories. I feel as though I have become that legion. I am Master Dreamweaver, silent head of the Guild, and, unknown to the Guild, I am also Ela, Master Dreamweaver, head of the Rebellion. The Guild has been fighting the Rebellion for fifteen years, shortly after Edain was deeded to them. It frightens them that their settlements of the arts are under protest by children who work as their labourers, what the Guild calls apprenticing. We cannot make these other species understand dreamweavers are a species unto themselves. By putting dreamweaver children under stress, they are endangering not only us, but themselves. As the children die off, we absorb their masses. So, I weave a complicated tapestry to bring the two to an understanding, which may create resolution.

But for now, I must weave a tapestry unrelated to this. I must incarnate a tale, spin a yarn, weave a dream.

This is the ultimate art—the art of storytelling, of dreamweaving. It is an exacting art. I use no canvas, no paint, no stone, no chisel. I am denied holography, photography—any graphic means. I deal with illusion, as do all other art forms, but I am denied an opportunity to make that illusion visual. My canvas is the mind, and each interpretation of my story is unique. And yet I create images, sights, sounds, scents so real my listeners are spellbound by my art. Mine is the purest form of creation. I create reality.

Here it comes—a tale, a tapestry, a dream I will weave: a star, yellow, a living star that thinks and watches. There, see it grow, so tiny at first, now larger. Warmth, it has warmth, and a scent like…like flint. It watches the little lives on its planets. How quickly they burst and fade. There is one it sees—a male child, suddenly a man, born on Setebos and disfigured so that he is lovely in a hurtful way. It watches how he turns his face to it, like a heliotrope following its path across his world. It longs to embrace him….

But the other images I create waver. And there is the rebellion to consider. I cannot weave a tapestry, not a real, living tapestry without jeopardizing what we have all worked so hard to gain.

There, my lovely sun has died. It warms me no more. Only the fragrance of it remains…here, in this desolation.

I will not mourn. Soon, not long, and I will again be able to complete a tapestry. I mustn't fail.

I will, instead, watch our friend Ambassador Tine. Setebos wishes an Edain envoy, that is sure. Gain Setebos and my work will be almost complete. Setebos, where some realities evolve over spans of time, and others burst and die in moments, where the evolutionary summit is held by the overlooked and undervalued Calibans, a species considered horrific by some, predatory by others, ignorant brutes by others yet, bound to their planet through benevolent symbiosis with a spore that protects Caliban life forms from a highly radioactive star. The trade-off, and there is always a trade-off, is a question of cosmetics, and in art the question of beauty is always

     Caliban

subjective. It is that very discussion that makes Tine a potentially powerful ally.

Gain Setebos and there is hope I can achieve what is necessary to keep us all alive.

If I do that, then once again I can weave.

TINE QUICKLY summoned a floater, heading back to Ela's home so he could check on the sweep's status. Tylan's anger still vibrated through him, and he was aware he'd sustained several cuts and scrapes from the flying debris of the nepanthaloid's forest. He'd been pelted with fruits and nuts, some the size of his head and just as hard, branches and, as he'd leapt onto his floater, a gargantuan tree had crashed down where he'd stood. Plainly Tine had uncovered something, and not at all to Tylan's pleasure. Enough to kill him? Certainly looked that way. But why? And what was the Guild hiding?

He stole a glance over-shoulder as he sped away, watching the entire floating forest gyrating as though it would tear apart. None of it made sense. He remembered the birthing trees before he'd left home, the screams in sympathy with Setebos' rhythm of life, the way he and his brood gorged and giggled on the bounty of the day. These things he knew. These things he could understand.

But this? This was strange and nonsensical, beyond understanding. Yet he must try to understand what was going on here, make some sense of their strange customs, their strange society. This very manufactured and carefully maintained society.

He could only hope the sweep had been into Ela's home and garnered enough of a sonic harvest to give him some clues. If he could elicit such a reaction from Tylan, surely matters in the Master Dreamweaver's home would prove it the hive of plots.

When he landed at the edge of Ela's clouds, the same rug-rider he'd travelled with before popped into view. Tine flinched.

"Master Ela wishes to meet you in the work-warrens."

More confusion. More nonsense. "Work-warrens?"

"The place that creates all of Edain's industry."

Creates industry. There was a clue there, something deeper than the phrase indicated. But what it was he couldn't quite grasp. Again, he asked himself why Jabod risked all by sending in Tine? Why use an unseasoned and back-planet agent? "Why?" And it was a question directed to more than the rug-rider.

"She thought you would like to see how Edain is run."

Tine glanced up at the clouds of Ela's home. If the sweep were still inside there, his detour would give the drone a little more time. And it would be useful to know who provided for all the artists on this utopian planet.

Without further thought, Tine boarded the rug, dug in his claws, and yielded to that unsettling mode of transport. Nothingness again seized him. Ela was the next reality.

She stood before a nondescript building, grey, all real material construction and by virtue of its plainness an oddity and a shout in this city of artifice.

She, also, was dressed in a nondescript semblance of garments, some sort of trousers and tunic as grey and inconspicuous as the building in front of which she stood. Tine didn't trust her. Of that he was certain. He thought of Aganth's honest face, of her clear and artless words.

The silence of the moment struck him. And the stillness. There were no citizens here. None. Overhead no floaters zipped by. No conveyors criss-crossed the plain street which appeared to be nothing more than packed earth, not unlike the floor of his home. And then through the silence he could barely detect a soft susurration, like waves, or wind in leaves. Rustling. Whispers. Echoes of things he was sure he should hearken and couldn't quite grasp.

Ela nodded smoothly to the creature on the rug when Tine slid off. Both rug and creature popped away. She smiled at Tine. He felt no amity.

"I'm glad you decided to join me."

"I had a choice?"

"Of course, Ambassador."

He nodded to where the rug-rider had been. "Who or what is that?"

"That is my thread."

Thread...tapestry....

"Something you wove."

She frowned. "Of course. What else?"

What else indeed, he wondered. Why not create a chauffeur for him?

His gaze swung over the building before them. It again struck him odd there were no travellers here, that the building was so plain, unobtrusive, as though to discourage interest.

Work-warrens?

"I thought you might like to see how this dome of Maxta is run." She gestured to the building.

Tine nodded, searching for some evidence of a door. His question was answered when Ela palmed the stone. A slab slid aside, unleashing sound that chilled him. Darkness lurked there. Tine remembered the orgy. He shuddered, stepped back. She stepped forward into the hole. Panic nipped his skin. His gaze bounced over his surroundings. What else was there to do but follow? He was, after all, here to find out what had happened to the Gelt Ambassador.

He stepped into darkness. Sound swallowed him. Had Ela not touched his shoulder, he would have never heard her speak of a direction. The stone door slid back into place, snuffing the light. Cautiously, he followed.

Only a few paces further the darkness seemed a studded swath of the universe, as if one small section had been carved out of space and bound to this building, bodies aglow with the art of weaving, each shining a solitary warmth which warmed no one. It was something he found beautiful, and equally painful. In all of this beauty there was no sound of laughter, no emotion, nothing to give dimension to what he saw. Each glowing body turned in a world of their own, their own voices their only company. Nothing penetrated. There was only the glow from the dreamweavers and the chanting voices, monotonous, dull, lapping one over the other in sibilance.

"What is this?" he finally asked.

“This is a work-warren.”

“Work-warren? But there’s no work being done.”

She laughed. “But there is. There is work, doing. These are all dreamweavers—children who are serving their apprenticeship by creating all of the industry and survival Maxta requires.”

All? These few? His gaze fired back to the glowing bodies—static, utterly motionless but for their pulsing light. Only their voices created motion, droning on and on and on like some purgatorial chant.

Children?

Were these children?

“And the other domes?” he asked.

“All sustained in this manner. Every dome has a work-warren.”

He moved, walked among them, a lightless satellite swinging around their power. These were indeed children. The lack of laughter seemed heinous. These children should have been bright with play, laughter carolling around them like an anthem. There should have been rough and tumble, tests of wit and strength and challenges into the rites of passage.

But there was none. Only these few, raining their stories out into darkness, sending tendrils of reality through walls, into Maxta.

“What kind of abomination is this?” he demanded.

There was some odd pose to her face when he turned to her, some odd tremor in her voice when she answered, “We, each of us, have our own reality. Theirs can be no worse than another’s.”

“This is art? This is your grand vision of freedom of expression?”

"You don't know all the facts, Ambassador."

"Then enlighten me."

"I'm not sure you'd understand."

"Try me."

He watched, his claws unsheathing and sheathing, one of the children who was caught in the thrall of weaving. Before he realized what was happening, a figure divided from the child, her voice rising to a screech that ground against Tine's teeth. The figure attacked him without provocation, without warning. Tine parried, struck, reacting to his body's instinct to survive. The child's screech bled into a howl. The character she wove vanished. A flame like a blue tongue licked at her belly, exploded, shrouded her in a conflagration—all of this so rapid Tine was still recovering from his attack. In the next moment, the girl collapsed, a charred corpse. A cloud rose over her, surged toward Ela who again seemed to swallow the thing against her will.

There in the darkness the other children continued to weave their tapestries without once pausing to glance at the girl who now lay smouldering on the floor.

He would watch no more. He turned and fled back into the light of the streets, letting his flight take him where it would. Anywhere but in that nightmare.

It may occur to you, during this trial, that dreamweavers who are capable of creating realties are a species dangerous in their power. Think nothing of the kind. They are in thrall to what they are, interwoven into one another's lives so intricately they find it difficult to discern what has been woven, and what exists as a part of the natural order of things. They are no different than any other species throughout the universe. All of us are thrall to what we are. There is no escape. They are bound by the realities they create, be that reality a paradise or a purgatory.

THE EDAIN TRIAL, JURY ADDRESS FROM
THE DREAMWEAVER COMMISSIONER TINE.

FINALLY TINE stopped. He stood, back to a wall of citron-coloured crystal, his eyes closed to the horror of what he'd seen. It mattered little to him at that moment how many glances he garnered. These people were little worthy of his respect.

To use children like that!

He remembered his own brood, the inviolate compact of trust he and Aganth worked so hard to nurture. The galaxy was a hard place, particularly on Setebos, so it was out of necessity the brood alphas warded their young. There was safety in numbers, and if the numbers were strong, worked together as a unit, they guaranteed the safety and strength of them all. They could survive. They could flourish. And it was the children who were the key. Safeguard the children; the future was assured.

He closed his eyes on his surroundings, remembering his home, remembering Aganth's wrinkled, warted face, the way her canines flashed when she smiled, the way oil oozed from her pores, and he realized he loved her for it. Loved her still. Was as bound to her and Setebos as if the spore never left him. Symbiosis was more than the spore. It was building a life together, facing hardship and bounty with equanimity. Being a part of one another, light and dark, strength and softness, instinct and intellect.

Why had he ever left? Why had he ever thought he should forfeit all he had simply to witness what he had?

To use children like that!

It was only when the air popped he finally opened his eyes. Shock unhinged him for a moment. Once more the rug-rider hovered before him. He did nothing to conceal the rage in his hands, allowing his claws to unsheathe, the oils to drip unchecked across his hide. He assumed a killing stance, ready to lash out with hooves and claws and teeth, and rip the throat out of this creature who dared intrude upon his pain.

"Are we going somewhere?" he growled. He was aware of how dangerous his voice sounded.

The Wart jigged on the carpet, its arms waving. "Master Ela needs you!" it squeaked. "Come! Come!"

Need him? Now she needed him? *She rapes me, shows me this abomination, and now she needs me?* "And what if I don't go?"

"Your mission will fail."

Tine grinned. There was nothing pleasant in his smile, he knew. It would be all canines. For once he was pleased with what Setebos made him. "You're very persuasive for a thread."

"No time for games! Get on! Get on!"

This piqued his curiosity more than he could ignore. He barely had time to settle when they dematerialized.

When reality congealed around him once more, the air itself seemed to wail, sinister, hopeless. Despite himself, Tine shuddered. His glanced over the cloud of Ela's home. Instead of the pastel vapour, the cloud was slate grey and vitriolic green, churning as if building for tempest. He knew that kind of cloud, what it could wreck.

That unearthly wail ripped through the cloud again, vapour spewing like volcanic ash. The rug bucked in the aftershocks. Tine's claws sank into its fibres.

"Quickly! Quickly!" the Wart shrieked, almost transparent now.

Tine shifted his gaze to his guide. The creature wavered several times, fading into and out of focus. Tine found himself plummeting toward the towers of the city, only to be rescued moments later.

"What's going on?" he demanded, regaining his wits.

"Quick! She needs you! Go before I fade!"

Something primal moved him. His hooves

disappeared into the cloud just as both Wart and rug vanished. There wasn't time for speculation. Winds battered him. Breath was almost an impossibility and it was then the unique construction of his body shoved him into action. He felt the heat of adrenaline. His skin felt slick with oil. Before he even realized he was moving, he sprinted through Ela's rooms, now battling ectoplasmic charges and a suffocating wind.

When he found her he went numb. She was contorted into a parody of tragedy, her limbs thrashing at the vaporous figures that entangled her like a net of veils. To his horror, a blue flame flickered from her belly.

"Ela!" he shouted, letting savagery take his tone. "Stop weaving!"

"Oh-h-h...not another...." She groaned. Her eyes were blank, unfocused.

Tine leapt and grabbed her by the shoulders. "I'm real, Ela. Stop weaving!"

For a moment she seemed to see him. She smiled. There was something utterly helpless in that smile, something out of character with the aloof Master he'd met only yesterday. All he could think of was Moishen's message.

"Tine...."

The threads around them vanished. Ela screamed then, batting at the flame. Now it had all her attention. Already it threatened to consume her. She mouthed silent words, her gaze on Tine. There was an ocean of misery in her eyes. He remembered how his oil had smothered Moishen's flame. Before she lost consciousness, he yanked her body against his, allowing his warts to open and seal their flesh together. She sagged against him. But he held her upright until he was sure the flame died.

His jaw ached from grinding his teeth. So much pain! And the stink! He swallowed from a dry mouth, his tongue feeling like sand.

"Ela...." He lifted her limp body into his arms. His contempt of her fled under the weight of his pity; if this was the price of her art, then he could do nothing but pity her for her bonds.

She still hung unconscious from his limbs. He debated whether to leave her and flee back to the IPCIB liner. This mission was going anything but routinely, and still he'd come no closer to discovering what had happened to the Gelt Ambassador. Agreed it had only been two days. He reconsidered. Punishment for abandoning a mission was severe, and he had no wish to endure that. Cowardice. No, there was the matter of Ela. And if he were honest, he wanted to go home.

She moaned, helpless in his arms. He thought of Aganth, his cruelty, the way he'd thrown aside his life with her, his brood, everything that should have given definition and meaning to his existence all for the pursuit of sensation. He'd already abandoned one responsibility. Would he now abandon two? Was Ela his responsibility?

"Make me a bed for her," he commanded the walls, unsure if the result would be from technology or some dreamweaver child held as slave to Edain's needs. At the moment it didn't matter. He had to do something about Ela.

Vapour coagulated near his hooves. He dumped her unceremoniously onto the bed, and then considered whether to seek out a medic for her. No one had seemed particularly concerned about Moishen. And no one had come to investigate the disturbance in Ela's home, settled now though it was. Why was that? Why had no one come to investigate?

Unsure of her circumstances and the customs of Edain, he opted against any outside interference. He surveyed her carefully. Reassured by what he saw, he leaned toward her.

"Ela," he said. "Ela, can you hear me?"

Her eyes snapped open. Tine couldn't remember seeing such terror.

"How do you feel?" he asked.

She inhaled sharply. "Weak…afraid…a little numb, I think." Her fingers pressed against her belly, her eyes widening. There was only a slight blister there. "I didn't combust."

"You were expecting to?"

Her eyes closed. "Weavers always combust when they lose control."

"I think you have some explaining to do."

She nodded. "How long have I been out?"

"A few minomes…er, minutes." He sensed questions within questions. "Why?"

"I have to get out."

He folded his arms across his chest. "Again, I'm asking why?"

"You wouldn't understand," she snapped, rising on her elbows. "You'll be safe back at your hotel. Don't stay here." She lifted her legs over the edge of the bed and slid to her feet. "Deny any involvement with me, Ambassador, for your own safety." She leaned toward him, her face a portrait of worry. "If you've any brains in that Caliban skull, you'll go back to your backwater planet and lobby to keep the Guild out."

This was something Tine hadn't expected. "And what if I decide you need an ally?"

She laughed bitterly, stinging Tine. "You're a fool, and an admirable one at that. But I can't allow you to do that. My problems aren't yours."

"A Guild envoy to see you, Master Ela," a voice said, bringing a flash of anger across Ela's face. Tine hadn't ever witnessed such hot disgust.

She threw him a glance. She straightened. "Show them to the west third altitude, serve them beverages, and tell them I'll be with them momentarily."

"As you wish, Master Ela."

She returned her attention to Tine, grimness replacing anger. "You're involved now, Ambassador, just as you wanted. I'm sorry. You may regret this."

Again she became the cool dreamweaver he'd first met, that unreadable curve to her lips. Gold light draped her figure. As Moishen's aura had expanded, so did Ela's until it divided; briefly, Tine thought he'd hallucinated. It seemed as if Ela walked out of her body. Then he realized; she'd woven her double, plainly a decoy for the Guild envoy. But why? Her clone stared at her. Ela nodded. The double turned and left. Just as rapidly, Ela's luminosity died.

"You can weave without speaking," he said, needing to say the obvious. He remembered Moishen, all those children, that incessant drone of words on words on words.

Her smile was self-effacing. "Better than what you've just witnessed. I can weave small tapestries without incandescence…periodically. That's why I'm Master Dreamweaver.

"Now, Ambassador, you're going to have to be my hostage for awhile. Do exactly as I say and you won't come to any harm." As she had many times previously, she didn't wait for his response. "Wart," she said. "I need you."

The air popped. There, in the middle of sound, appeared the rug-rider. Tine's suspicions about Ela's abilities were realized. The magnitude of her craft left him uneasy, echoed by the lingering darkness of the clouds.

With a gesture, she indicated he should board. When he settled, she followed. Again, Tine shuddered in the void between destinations, wondering just what Ela's mysterious and erratic behaviour meant. He had the feeling she was playing a clever, albeit dangerous, part. Had he been in the company of a suspect all this time? Was Ela responsible for the Gelt Ambassador's disappearance?

The brilliance of the never-ending Edain day burst upon him, leaving him feeling exposed and vulnerable. His gaze darted around, catching the amethyst paving stones and the bright shaft of a laser-run.

"You have a choice now: go back to your liner or submit as my hostage," Ela said. There was no menace in her tone, only weariness.

He shot her a glance.

Caught! She knows! "I can't," he said.

She arched a brow.

Can I trust her? "I'm not what you think."

"I haven't time for this."

Tine shifted his focus. "Are you running from the Guild because you're a rebel?"

There was no emotion on her face. "Yes. But you shouldn't have asked. I'll have to do something about you now."

Again, he was struck by the lack of menace in her tone. This was simply business.

"Not necessarily," he answered, his gaze flicking to people moving through the plaza. "As you suspect, I'm an IPCIB active on assignment to Edain." That he left out details about the Gelt Ambassador didn't bother him. He needed Ela as a passport into the rebel colony.

She mouthed a silent, "What?"

He wrinkled his face into a shrug. "IPCIB thought something unusual was going on down here, what with your reports of a crimeless society and all." He gestured to himself. "Enter the Sctebian Ambassador."

"Why should I believe you?"

He could hear the danger in her voice. Tine knew he'd have to answer precisely.

"There's no reason why you should," he said. "But I'm asking you to."

Now would come the moment where decisions would determine his life. It had been a long time since he had experienced that kind of danger, the kind of danger that was lethal, filled with cool reason—a predatory kind of instinct that had nothing to do with malice.

The last time had been during the prenuptial rituals of the Calibans, specifically during *his* prenuptial ritual. He'd been pitted against Aganth in a test of wits. Time had turned slowly. There hadn't even been any blows, no weapons, and yet the air had shuddered with violence. His fate had balanced on carefully tendered words, costly words.

He watched Ela's face for signs. She was still unreadable, distant, terribly alien...wonderful in her danger. Decision swept over her frame. She smiled.

"Then I'll watch your vulnerability with care, Tine. Truth and time have a way of testing."

Crisis passed. Tine felt himself withholding a sigh. That would have revealed a weakness. What he didn't need now was anything to compromise his situation. His mission stood on the verge of completion, he was sure. Nothing would jeopardize that.

For Ela it seemed matters had also headed on a different course. Her demeanour seemed less like the assassin and more like the dreamweaver.

"You'll be branded now," she warned him. "It may mean you'll never be able to return to Maxta."

"Why?"

She gestured widely. "This city—Maxta—this is the centre of all Edain, at least, the Edain the UOoP know. The Guild will watch for you at every portal. They'll accuse you of allying with the rebels."

"A calculated risk," he answered. "I assume I'll be able to return to my liner from a run wherever we're going."

Her laughter denied him. "We're going into the Skeins, Tine. The Skeins. The Weaverlands. My home."

His question died on his tongue. Ela commanded

Wart to a new destination, and instantly nothingness seized them. The sensations of that special kind of travel completely unnerved him. This time the interval was extended, utterly barren. Even time-sense died. He wondered if he'd ever be able to return to Setebos. The fact he even thought about that set his teeth to the grind. Setebos had been something from which he'd been attempting to flee.

Why would I want to go back?

He swallowed. *There's every reason why I'd want to go back.*

He was thinking about that when they burst upon a world of sienna and carnelian rocks, almost bloody in hue. Tine felt hurtled back to the landscape of Setebos, a place where a person could drown in austerity, barrenness, mystery during the dry years. He wondered just how much Jabod knew about Edain. It would seem the Commissioner had chosen the perfect candidate to investigate this planet. And why had details about the undomed regions been omitted from everything he read? *Uncharted. Uninhabitable.*

"Where are we?" he asked, looking over to Ela.

Any further inquiry was aborted. From the look on Ela's face he doubted he would receive any useful information. She was lost in a moment of reverie. Bittersweet was the only way he could describe her face, a look compounded with loss, longing, loathing.

Her voice was hollow when she answered, "We're on the border of the Skeins. This is the real Edain, the Edain that existed before the planet was deeded to that pack of revolutionary artists." She turned her face toward him. Tine wanted to weep for the pain on her face. "No one knew we were here. We couldn't make ourselves known. And then when we figured out how to make ourselves known, it was too late. They don't believe us."

She slid off the carpet, gesturing for Tine to follow, which he did. The ground beneath his hooves felt solid, real, something with which he was familiar—a baked land of pounded dirt. He turned and looked back to the distant bubble of Maxta. It was then he realized the fleshy hue of the earth came from sunset. The yellow disk in a crimson sky made him feel unreal. Already the plastic world of Maxta had distorted his perspective.

On the opposite horizon, where the sky was a wine-purple, a toothy ridge of rock rose. Even from this distance he could tell it was an ancient echo of volcanoes.

"That way's Maxta?" he asked at length, nodding toward the west and the sun where the bubble glistened.

She nodded.

"And that way?" He nodded to the east.

"The Skeins." She shuddered. Tine wondered why. "You can go back to my memory now, Wart," she said softly, almost as if she were saying farewell to a beloved friend. Both carpet and curious creature faded.

"And now?" Tine asked.

Ela looked to the east, as if turning toward a terrible god. "We walk. It's a two-day trip to the first loom. Nothing will be easy from here on. The Guild soon will send out a small scout to look for us. I won't be able to control that thread of me for long...not out here. But they won't dare follow us at night." Her smile was grim. "They don't like the Skeins at night." Slowly, Ela turned back to him. "You won't like the Skeins at night. It's a time when dreamweavers think, and when we think, things happen. Be sure you have a firm grip on reality from now on, Tine. I'll be able to do very little to help."

There was warning in her. But try as he might he couldn't place that warning. Of what should he be cautious? How could her weaving possibly harm him, and then he asked a question he would regret in days to come, a question that would haunt him and feed his fears.

"When we orgied, was that a tapestry?"

Her spidery fingers traced the lumps on his shoulder. "Maybe you'll find a way to survive with us, Tine. You're very perceptive for an outsider. Yes, that was a tapestry. Only I was real. I thought a yarn of excess would please you. It seems not." She withdrew her fingers. "You're a curiosity."

The grin on his face was superficial, placed there only to smooth the moment. "Then that makes two of us." He gestured to the land before them. "I believe we have a night of travelling, Ela. My hide is bound by your countenance...." He let the Caliban aphorism dangle.

That night Tine contemplated the moons while Ela's images foamed in their wake.

Many of the clues as to the nature of dreamweavers are hidden in the Genesis of the Skeins. Like all myth-literature, it has a foundation in truth.
REPORT FROM THE COMMISSION ON DREAMWEAVERS

TYLAN SENSED them all, these key members of the Edain Guild. He sensed their tension. He sensed their alarm. He also sensed their fear. When a nepanthaloid like Tylan summoned a guest, it was rarely to exchange courtesies.

All three guests were humanoid. Hogan the Master Photographer and Jen the Master Holographer were huddled together as these twins often were, their hands twining and untwining as if they might communicate through the sensation of touch. These two would be no trouble, Tylan was sure. It was Athran there, the Master Painter, standing ensconced in a cascade of ferns, who would delight in finding a flaw in everything said.

It mattered little. The outcome would be the same. Once Luther from IPCIB arrived, they'd see that Tylan had been right all along to suspect Ela. They should have listened to his warnings that she was a rebel. He hadn't met a dreamweaver yet he could trust.

"What is all this about?" That was Hogan, the Master Photographer. Tylan could identify him more from the rise in carbon dioxide rather than through auditory means.

Tylan felt the spasm pass through him, a prelude to the voice interpreter. "We'll wait for Luther."

"I think we should be briefed," Jen said.

"We'll wait for Luther."

There was no disputing his authority, he knew.

Within moments the house security announced Luther's arrival, and only moments after that a yellow bird escorted the IPCIB representative to where they all waited. For a human Luther was old, bent, his rheumy eyes like bloodshot wax. Were it not for their glitter it would be easy to overlook Luther's intelligence. He waved off their greetings.

"What's all this about?" he said.

"Seems that's a question we're all asking." Athran, the Master Painter, this time. "Do break the suspense."

Tylan wouldn't be threatened. "You were sure to cover yourself?"

"Of course I was," Luther answered. "IPCIB hasn't found out about my involvement with the Guild yet. I don't intend to let them know now."

"And the captain of the IPCIB liner?"

"What about her?"

"Does she know you're here?"

"She'd have to, wouldn't she? I wouldn't be here otherwise."

"Aren't you taking an unwarranted risk?" Jen asked.

"Sometimes I think the Guild's monopoly is on stupidity, not the arts."

"The captain's with us," Tylan answered.

"Now let's cut the crap," Luther said. "What's this meeting all about?"

"Ela's gone."

"So? It wouldn't be the first time she's disappeared for awhile."

"With the Caliban Ambassador."

Even without eyes Tylan could sense their mouths gaping, feel their shock like an angry wave.

"You're sure?" Hogan asked.

"Positive. She wove a thread of herself to take her place. It dissolved. The Caliban Ambassador's nowhere to be found."

"Maybe she's taken him hostage?"

"That seems unlikely."

"Why should it be unlikely?" Jen asked.

"Why would she take him hostage when she'd shown him the work-warrens? I'd say that was a little bold, even for Ela."

"You've proof?"

"I saw the Ambassador fleeing from the work-warrens," Athran said. "There can be no other explanation but that Ela took him there." He gestured to the ferns behind him where a child cowered in the shadows. "I always did find it odd that these animals would say nothing of her—she who is an example to them all of what a dreamweaver should be."

Tylan felt Luther's cold humour. "I suggest we interrogate this thing you've brought with you."

"I've already asked the child if he saw her."

"I doubt you could glean anything useful from him."

"At least I keep my subjects alive."

The child whimpered Ela's name. A look passed between Jen and Hogan.

"Enough of this," Tylan said. "Bring the child out. Let Luther do what he's best at."

Athran shrugged, turned, pulled the child out of the ferns and placed the boy before Luther.

"Tell me," Luther said. "What was Master Ela doing in the work-warrens?"

"I don't know."

"You saw her didn't you?"

Tylan could hear the boy nod, sensed the child had his face turned down to the ground.

"What was she doing?" Luther asked.

"Ela—"

"She's not here." He shook the child. "Answer me. What was she doing?"

The boy sobbed.

"Answer me, damn you!"

"Very good, Luther," Athran said. "That's a very effective technique."

"I'll show you effective." Luther unclipped a small cylinder from his belt, flicked a button. A light gleamed on the device, solely for the benefit of the user. Tylan could feel the octobots in there, knew the destructive power of that infinitesimally invisible bead of liquid Luther would dispense. "I can cut apart your face and rearrange it any way I like. I'd suggest you answer me. What was Master Ela doing?"

The boy shook his head, whimpering Ela's name as if she were his only salvation. In the next moment his whimpering bled to a scream, high, shrill. Tylan could smell the open, plasticized flesh, sensed it from mouth to eye. Still the child said nothing of Ela. Luther dispensed another mote of horror. This time words tumbled from the child's mouth in a torrent, his body glowing until the things of which he spoke spun through the leafy arena in which they all stood. The answer he gave told them nothing.

"There was light and there was darkness and there was a dreamweaver to spin the two together into a tapestry. And the tapestry woven was of dreams. And the dreams were of weaving."

Luther acted again. The boy's shoulders dripped down his arms, and still his voice was audible, a clear, high defiance.

"For thirty days and thirty nights the weaving went on, and she was tired and without drink or succour, and yet under her fingers the tapestry grew. With light she wove flesh, and with darkness she wove mystery. And the mystery became the thoughts of flesh. That which was neither light nor darkness became that upon which flesh would stand, the thing which would give flesh succour and rest and drink of which she knew nothing...."

Luther snarled, poking and poking now in what seemed a bizarre dance, back and forth, each touch releasing octobots which lay open the boy's face until it was tatters, his arms like scarves which now spun out and formed figures and landscape.

"And when the thirty days and thirty nights had passed, she cast off her tapestry and left the loom barren. Through the frame shone the unused skeins. By their light she at last came to rest, spreading her tapestry beneath her.

"While the weaver of dreams slept, the flesh of her dreams stirred, breaking the bonds of warp and weft; with his own fingers he repaired the tapestry. Tired, he lay beside the weaver who had woven him.

"But the spell of weaving was still upon her, and dreaming she wove, she lay with the dream of flesh and knew him. And from the dream of flesh, flesh was created."

"Stop it!" Luther shouted, slashing now at the boy's body. Athran, Jen, and Hogan echoed that warning, directing it at Luther. Tylan only trembled.

Still the boy wove his tapestry, his light brilliant, his words like thunder.

"The dreamweaver and her lover adored the child of dreams, and taught her how to spin their yarns. Often they would exchange tapestries after the evening meal, by the fragrant light of a fire, and as time went on, this became their custom.

"And as time went on, the child of their dreams learned to weave also, tapestries of such beauty and power that they, also, were a reality. Each reality fed her. Afraid for their child of dreams, the dreamweaver and the dream of flesh bade her weave no more. But how could she not weave?"

That question drummed through the forest.

Tylan asked himself that, willing Luther to stop his bloodless interrogation of this child. But he wouldn't be stopped. Somehow the child remained standing although his flesh ran like ribbons. A flame spouted from the gore of his belly, a flame of blue, hot and consuming. Still he wove his tapestry.

"So it was that one night, when the dreamweaver and the dream of flesh slept, the child of dreams awoke and wove, wove so quickly and deftly that heat grew under her fingers. The heat grew, expanded, flashed into incandescence, and still she wove until she was bright, brilliant, effulgent. Her light stirred the dreamweaver and the dream of flesh. Afraid, they fled. But there was nowhere the child of dreams couldn't reach them.

"Even to this day she shines. And still they cannot look upon her."

The child combusted completely, a pillar of blue flame. Overhead a cloud formed, sighed, and when the carnage ended only Tylan remained unaffected, his fleshly leaves folding over the meat left from the child.

Define for me intelligence. Does intelligence require that a being be a toolmaker? What if that society has no need of tools? Are they, then, unintelligent? Does intelligence require a being to contemplate itself? What if we have no way to communicate with that being? Are they, then, unintelligent because of our lack? Does intelligence require a being to be able to reason? What if that being's reasoning is so far removed from ours that to us it is non-reasoning? Are they, therefore, unintelligent? Define for me, then, dreamweavers.

THE EDAIN TRIAL, JURY ADDRESS FROM THE
DREAMWEAVER COMMISSIONER TINE

THAT FIRST night they covered twenty miles, although to Tine it seemed closer to a hundred. Journeying hadn't been easy. It hadn't been easy because Ela wove, and wove, and wove, to the point of what Tine assumed was obsession. He asked himself if this was the experience of the Skeins; a place, he was sure, all of his preconceptions and realities would have no meaning.

The air around him had been thick with characters, some known, some unknown, and some simply bizarre. Ela seemed to be able to reach into his mind and incarnate people he'd long ago forgotten, and even some he wished he could forget. People like Aganth.

At times, he'd stumbled in Ela's wake, shocked by what he'd seen. There, in the light of seven moons, had been his brood, twenty-nine children he loved, and missed, and from whom he longed to have forgiveness. Tine wouldn't confront the fact he also longed for Aganth's forgiveness.

Only when the threads faded did he realize that Ela had been weaving, and that his family was still on Setebos.

By the time dawn was pink on the horizon, he wasn't sure about what was real and what was not. All his senses were serrated. At every sound he flinched, sure someone else came to share their path.

Exhausted, not from their long night's walk, but from their long night of illusion, he squatted. Ela paced on, seemingly ignorant of her hostage until he called to her. A shudder took her dementia. She turned. In that moment, she seemed to be the stuff of legends to him, a creature of mystery bathed in gold morning light, a creature of tragedies.

"It's time to rest, Ela," he said, thinking how real his voice sounded. It was the first real thing of which he could be sure in many hours.

She only nodded and paced back toward him. When she knelt beside him her gaze was piercing the horizons, searching, perhaps hunting.

"I lost control of the thread of me last night," she said suddenly, her tone flat.

Tine's attention shot to her. "That doesn't surprise me."

Her brow arched.

"You wove so much last night it would be impossible to keep control of that thread."

"I keep telling you, Tine, I'm a Master Dreamweaver. Although the title is costly, it's not without power. Didn't it ever occur to you it's me you should have been investigating, not Tylan?"

"The thought occurred to me. In fact, I've speculated that perhaps you're a double agent with both the Guild and the rebels."

"I'm not quite that treacherous, or selfish. No, a dreamweaver can't be selfish. That path leads to destruction. Everything I've done has been for what the Guild calls the rebels. I've spun threads into tapestries so elaborate it would awe you. But you'll find evidence of all that when we reach the Skeins."

Her gaze swung back to the west where Maxta lay. "The Guild will have sent out scouts by now, real scouts, but at least I've gained us a night's start."

"What do you mean real scouts?"

"Real scouts—flesh and blood people."

"There's something else?"

"Thread scouts, the scouts the children in the work-warrens weave to gather other children from the borderlands."

He shuddered.

She turned back to Tine. "You'll sleep for a few hours and then we'll continue. With any luck, we'll reach the Skeins by dawn tomorrow, and the Guild's scouts will go insane tonight." She smiled. "Yes, I think you may be able to adjust to the dreamweavers, Tine. You seem quite aware of reality at this moment. Usually, the first night in the borderlands drives anyone but a dreamweaver over the precipice of reality.”

“Was last night a test?”

“A test? In some respects, but not the way you think. Last night wasn’t preplanned.”

“Then why did you weave all night?”

She smiled that distant smile. “It’s what dreamweavers do out here. It’s the dreamweavers who are the rebels. It’s the dreamweavers who are Edain. Edain, in our tongue, means Skein.”

“You mean the dreamweavers were the ones who were here when the UOoP deeded Edain to the Guild?”

“Very good, Tine.”

“And you call murdering heads of state a just means to your end?” He growled, realizing he’d slipped. It was just that she unhinged him.

“Who said anything about murder?”

“All right, so I stretched the truth. IPCIB found a corpse of what they thought was the Gelt Ambassador.”

“So you’re Jabod’s person.”

“I’m my own person. But I work for Jabod, yes.”

“He told me about you.”

“You have him too?”

She nodded.

“Then who’s aboard the liner?”

“My thread.”

“Like the Gelt Ambassador?”

“You catch on quickly. What your IPCIB people found of the Gelt was a thread, not a body. There’s no proof those people were murdered.”

“Then where are they?”

She nodded to the east.

"In the Skeins?"

"Again, very good, Tine."

He gauged his next question carefully. "Are they insane?"

"Define sanity."

Tine shuddered with anger. "Don't play games, Ela. Are they insane?"

"Define sanity."

"Damn you!" He surged to his hooves. "Answer me!"

"I will if you define sanity for me."

He stared at her as if he could yank an answer out of her with his frustration. It was then he confronted the honesty in her face. She looked like the standard of innocence. She really wanted his definition of sanity. It occurred to him that he might find her definition startling.

"Are they capable, psychologically, of re-entering the societies they left?"

"Most," she said.

"The important ones? The ones who have power in the UOoP?"

"They all have power."

"How many do you have?"

"Thirty-one."

He swallowed.

Thirty-one! So many! Had Jabod any idea how serious this had become?

He would now, Tine was sure. But what could the Commissioner do out here?

His gaze flashed to Maxta.

"Do we need to set a watch?"

She shook her head. "If any of the scouts survived, they'll be insane, of no concern. The Guild will be afraid of me now."

Tine risked one more question. "Does the Guild realize the rebels are all dreamweavers?"

"They haven't a clue."

"Why not?"

That pitiful look came over her face again, a look that cried out her helplessness. "We can't make them understand what we are, that we're different."

"I don't understand."

"Of course not. You and I share a similar reality because of the isolation of our peoples. The Guild— they know nothing of what you and I know." She gestured to the ground. "Sweet dreams, Tine." She smiled at her own play on words. "My apologies your bed isn't softer."

"Just like home," he said and stretched out on the ochre earth.

The rest Ela afforded him was short. That did nothing to encourage Tine's discomfort. It was natural for him to nap. He was, however, ravenous, but she seemed not to consider the possibility of eating. Neither did Ela seem wearied by the long night of travel or the modicum of rest. That was just another bit of information he filed for reference.

The path to which Ela held them aimed straight for the escarpment ahead. As they came closer, Tine was able to make out shapes and colours. The hills were heavily forested. Colours in the foliage seemed strange. There was apparently not only a variety of greens, but purples that ranged from pale mauve to wine-red. Out of this mass of vegetation stabbed craggy cliffs of rose, bone-white and grey. These, combined with the white trunks of twisted trees reminded him of skeletons. Into what kind of graveyard was he going? Ela had been vague in her explanation of dreamweavers. Somehow he knew he was headed for a situation for which he could never be prepared.

Throughout the day Ela remained silent. At first that situation pleased Tine. He was able to speculate, particularly about what lay ahead and what he'd left behind. Tempest swelled around him and he knew he'd have to be ready. However, after the first few hours, Ela's silence irritated him to the point he dared ask questions.

"How extensive are the Skeins?"

She flinched. Tine realized he'd reeled her in from thought.

"We control everything undomed," she answered, her tone distant. "Including the borderlands."

"Was it an arbitrary decision on the part of the Guild where to settle?"

She smiled. "They think it was."

"But you stacked the odds."

"Of course. We had to place them in areas where they would be forced to isolate themselves. We're in the northern latitudes, and in another month this area will be dome deep in snow. That's when the endless night will begin."

"What's to prevent them from erecting domes

in the southern latitudes? I assume they know it's warm."

"Did your reports say it was?" she countered.

"No."

"Then you see how extensively we've woven our tapestries. The Guild won't build south of here because they believe it to be desolate."

"And is it?"

"Not in the least. Not in our terms."

"Your terms?"

"What we find of value and what the Guild finds of value are completely different."

"But if you have a thriving civilization, why haven't the UOoP satellites picked up any indication?"

"We don't live according to UOoP conventions. Do Calibans?"

He flinched. "We've been isolated from the other planets. It's natural that we'd live outside of popular conventions."

"Then you understand us very well."

Tine thrust his gaze to the ground. It angered him that she kept reminding him of his origins, and yet he felt that perhaps his origins were crucial to understanding the situation on Edain. That was when he stopped mid-stride. "The UOoP didn't know Calibans existed until twenty years after federation. That was before we allied."

"Exactly. And why were you overlooked?"

"We don't use conventional forms of architecture or settlement. If anything, we live as close to animal state as possible. Our environment predicates that."

"Then you see why we're similar."

"I've no proof of that yet."

She was some distance from him when she said, "You'll soon have more proof than you can handle."

Silence consumed them once more. And that suited Tine for the moment. He continued his observation of his surroundings, and its very strangeness echoed his mood.

Now they passed a few gnarled trees; Tine felt he was in a world parallel to Setebos. By the time they left the twelfth tree behind, he was aware that something moaned. It was almost as if the tree itself spoke as he passed beneath its disfigured limbs. Finally, he managed to locate the origin of the sound.

His gaze turned up to Ela. "Why are wind harps hanging in the trees?"

"A form of warning."

"To you or intruders?"

"Perhaps both."

What was that supposed to mean? "Does this mean we're coming close to the Skeins?"

"We're in the Skeins."

His gaze flashed around. "When?"

"When we passed the first tree. We only keep the borderlands stripped of vegetation."

"But you said it would take until tomorrow."

"Tomorrow before we reach the first loom."

"Loom?"

"Settlement."

The wind harp they passed moaned *lo-o-o-om*.

Some hours later they still walked, although there

had been no conversation. Hills rose in gentle waves, crowned in trees and carpeted in moss like jade velvet. Only the sound of the harps marked their passing. There seemed to be no birds to fill the air with sound, no songs, no joy. He thought of the work-warrens. No joy there. This place called the Skeins was an eerie place, like a dream. Even the moss on enormous boulders denied the reality of the stone beneath, and Tine felt as if he were being used because of his knowledge of illusion and harsh realities. Even so, that knowledge failed to help him.

Ela paused, her gaze swinging over her surroundings. "We'll rest here."

"Is it possible to find anything to eat?"

She nodded, gesturing to the vegetation around her. "Take your pick. There is little here you can't eat. Just remember not to consume anything yellow."

"Why not?"

"You'll die."

It bothered him that her manner had been so matter of fact. She had seemed so Caliban. Was it possible that two isolated civilizations could have paralleled one another? It was something he considered more and more. He found himself familiar with her harshness. It was a Caliban thing. And still, Setebos lay in him like a bitter fruit.

He nodded in acknowledgement of her warning, and while she pillowed her face on her arms, he foraged among ferns and roots, stuffing his face with both hands. Three eating cycles had been missed, and now all his body could do was scream at him with hunger.

His gorging took him out of sight of Ela, although he

hadn't realized. By dusk he found himself contentedly sated, however completely lost. He sprang upright. Nothing here was familiar and that further disoriented him. He was in a meadow of red-green ferns that nodded and bowed in a breeze. He looked up the hill to a crest of red, weeping trees. Below him a stream bounced over bone-white rocks that were shadowed with long, blue fingers cast from overhanging trees. Even from here he could make out the white eyes of ground flowers. But nowhere could he find Ela. Panic took him for a moment. Instinctively he rubbed the oil from his warts over his skin, thinking, preparing. What would he do if he couldn't find her? Would other threads find him in the night to test his sanity? He wasn't even sure he should call out. There could be unfriendly dreamweavers about. Ela had been vague about details.

Prudence dictated his actions. He turned back toward the stream, assuming that was the direction from which he'd come. It was farther than he thought. By the time he made it into the cover of the tall trees, night had completely taken the sky. It was even darker within the forest. His recent experiences with darkness left him in a well of fear.

Tine found a rock for his rump. A breeze stirred the harps into voice. The air seemed to be filled with chattering ghosts, and spray from the cascade in the stream dampened his skin, increasing his discomfort. If he could keep his head until first moonrise, he was sure he'd be fine. Then, guided by the moons, he'd set out to find Ela.

Although a sound plan, Tine quickly realized it was anything but sound in a place like Edain. Nothing could protect him from the derangement of the dreamweavers.

There, alone, unfamiliar with this strange place, he was attacked. He groaned when he hit the ground, desperate to shove this maniacal man from him. It seemed as if he won the contest too easily. When Tine vaulted to his feet, the man disappeared.

Another person replaced his attacker—this time a woman.

"Go home, Toad! Go home before you die!" She laughed through the maze of her hair, her long fingers reaching for him. Tine cringed away, screamed despite himself, turned and ran into the arms of yet another person.

Soon the woods were alive with people so real they denied his reasoning. Few were sane in their approach. Most who came to share the night with him taunted, throwing words as cutting as knives, and as the moons rose, his visitors abused not only his mind, but his body. Some came with clubs, or hands, or things that cut, pierced. Some simply came to fill his head with stories so fantastic he could only sit mesmerized while others hurt him. As the night bloomed, so did his tolerance wane. When a willowy woman with eyes like a cat's entered his world, he laughed hysterically, sure he'd hallucinated a rescue.

Ela glowed. From out of her body walked other creatures—some like her, some utterly foreign, and again Aganth and his brood shared the moons with him.

This is illusion, he told himself, grasping at reality. *I must keep telling myself this is all illusion. The only thing real is me.*

I'm real. I'm real. I'm real.

He felt his claws unsheathe, his canines bare in a grin he knew would be terrible. In the pale, cold light he smelled the oil on his skin.

I'm real.

He refused to look at what occurred around him. When someone spoke to him he refused to acknowledge. After a while he rocked as if he were cradled in an endless nightmare.

I'm real.

He mouthed silent words, staring blankly out into Edain's eerie world. Threads around him called out his name, touching him with both pain and pleasure. In several places he bled profusely from wounds too deep for his system to handle. Where he sat was slick with oil. But still he told himself of his own reality.

When at last dawn paled the sky, he wept into the palms of his hands. He could hear a voice wailing, and realized it was his own.

He felt fingers on his shoulders, shied away, thinking he was again deluged by threads. He grabbed wrists and yanked the woman to the ground, his claws sinking deeply into her pale flesh. Around him other threads vanished like veils of smoke.

"It's morning, Tine," Ela said, looking directly at him. "The night's over."

He growled lowly, baring his teeth. In a rage, he vaulted away from her and splashed into the stream, throwing waves onto his oily body. He felt as though he would never be clean of Edain, and he abraded his skin ruthlessly.

When Ela's hands touched him he sank into the icy water, letting currents foam around his thighs.

"Oh, no, no, no," he groaned, letting his tears fall. And then he wept as if he were a child, letting Ela cradle his leathery head on her shoulder.

"I'm sorry, Tine," she whispered. It sounded like an echo of the harps. "I didn't mean for last night to be that hard on you."

All he could gasp between his sobs was, "I'm real, Ela."

Her kiss on his brow was one of compassion. "Yes, Tine. You're real. You'll have no trouble now when we meet the rest of the dreamweavers."

And somehow Tine knew he'd passed the hardest test of his life.

BURNING FLESH. It was a stench Tine now knew with familiarity. It pushed him into panic; somewhere near, a dreamweaver combusted.

He launched to his hooves. Vaguely, he was aware that he ran, his legs pumping. He could even hear the tippety-tappety of his hooves hitting a hard surface. When he looked down he saw the yellow blur of stone sliding away.

How could he not be going anywhere? He pushed himself harder, but that brought him no nearer to that figure writhing in the bowl of a barren valley. It was as if he ran on a treadmill. All that energy and nothing resulted except that his system overloaded with adrenaline. That meant the spore was still healthy and active in his system. Jabod lied. Or was lied to. *Can't think about that now.* He had to get to that burning figure.

He felt the air change, felt it like pressure on his skin, felt his lungs working for oxygen that wasn't there. He swallowed air in great mouthfuls, stooped and bent, claws distended over his knees. He analyzed the change. There was an increase in hydrogen and helium here. That was the magic elixir of stars. It was also the magic elixir of dreamweavers, an elixir created as a result of the phenomenon of weaving.

How did I know that? There was nothing about that in anything he'd read. How did he know Edain's atmosphere was hydrogen and helium rich because of the dreamweavers? It was then he wondered if it was possible a protostar was developing here, on this planet, within this nebula, because of the dreamweavers?

He was sure it was impossible for something as large as a star to occur out of something as relatively miniscule as a dreamweaver. There simply wasn't enough mass. There wasn't enough gravitational force to cause fusion.

But if there were enough of them?

Nonsense.

What he did know was that to allow the process of weaving to accelerate beyond the limits of flesh was to allow spontaneous combustion to occur. It was almost like the creation of a star, except not on as large a scale.

Tine knew then he dreamed. He dreamed about Ela, about a situation that seemed like a vista involving both of them, spied through a keyhole. He knew he could observe. And he knew he could not participate. He was there to witness, no matter how badly it hurt him. The reality of that made the dream ominous.

His senses stretched in an effort of will, and that

will demanded a break in the dream. There was more here than he was capable of accepting. His eyes sprang open. His first vision was of Ela, pulsing with light like an incandescent insect. It occurred to him her glow was like a star's, albeit a very small star.

He swallowed hard. Nothing in any of the reports he'd read said anything about dreamweaver physiology, perhaps because no one considered that the dreamweavers weren't what they seemed. The fact they were luminescent while weaving could have been considered a delightful aside, a product of super-active psychic capabilities, even natural bioluminescence.

And then Tine considered that perhaps the dreamweavers were far more powerful than he suspected. Perhaps they were so powerful that they'd fixed reports to protect themselves. That supposition, however, assumed native Edains considered other species hostile, and Tine wasn't sure if Ela or any of her kind felt threatened by the Guild or the populace of the neighbouring solar system.

It was while he stared at her he remembered the orgy. Copulating with her had been torturous. There had been incredible heat, a sense of being sucked into her body. If stars could feel, he was sure he'd felt the way a companion star would when twinned with a black hole.

He wondered, as he knew had many scientists, what was inside a black hole.

What's inside Ela?

Tine sat up. He still studied her as she wove. The fact that her tapestries no longer threatened his reality reassured him. Unlike the previous nights, he was able to watch her create and in doing so he could take in data.

Tonight she seemed not to have an interest in incarnating his family. Her yarn was simple. She wove a weaver who only stared into the ubiquitous nothingness that was her universe. At first that was all that happened. And then, as if epochs compressed into minutes, both the weaver and her world changed. She glowed. It was almost as if gentle flames fanned around her, reaching like long, arcing fingers into the void. The fingers stretched, oscillating now as if they had transformed into orange serpents, then red, then beyond Tine's light perception. Heat became something intolerable, so intense Tine tasted it— acrid, arid. Its withering seared his skin, pinched his nostrils. Within the weaver's waving fingers of light bloomed other points of light so bright they pricked Tine's eyes. This bursting of brilliance erupted into a frenzy of activity. Effulgent flowers spun around one another, forming larger flowers with spiralling tentacles, each with a centre laden with yellow pollen, and these, in turn, swept in languorous arcs around the nucleus of the weaver. All of this rippled in rings lapping ever outward.

The tapestry tilted, shifting emphasis from this pool of stars to a ball coagulating at the weaver's feet. Images from the ball zoomed into close range. For a moment Tine felt his stomach lurch. Motion stopped. The scene he surveyed was uncannily familiar—a landscape forbidding in its barrenness, alluring in its mystery. There, in that austere world was a man, a man Tine knew was real, skin and bones and intelligence, but it was apparent the weaver thought the man nothing more than a thread.

Tine felt he had read all this somewhere before when the weaver in the tapestry lay herself beside the man on the desolate planet. He watched how the weaver-thread subtly changed her anatomy so that it was more and more compatible with the man's. When they discovered each other's bodies, Tine knew a child would result, and that child would be a girl, a girl powerful in the art of dreamweaving.

He was so mesmerized by Ela's tapestry that he didn't notice dawn. It was only when the threads vanished and her muffled sobbing replaced her art that he realized the night, also, vanished.

His insides knotted.

"What is it, Ela?" he asked, not unkindly. He wasn't prepared for emotion. He wasn't prepared for tears. She was always so distant, so cool, a creature so utterly unapproachable.

She only shook her head, shielding her face in her long-fingered hands.

"Are you in pain?"

Again she shook her head.

"Can I do anything?"

She dug the heels of her hands into her eyes. "No! You're not ready yet."

"Ready for what?"

She snapped up her head. Tine shrank under her gaze. There was something ancient there, something he felt he could never understand or encompass with the standards of his world.

"Ready for what you least expect," she answered

smoothly. She rocked back onto her heels and rose, her pale hair tossing behind her like a veil. "It's time to move."

"I'm hungry. You must be also. I haven't seen you eat a thing since we began."

He could hear the smile in her voice when she answered, "You can munch as we go, Tine. As for me—I'm not hungry."

Tine could do nothing but glare at her as she paced off ahead of him. He kept his arguments to himself. It was obvious Ela only gave him answers when she felt he was ready to accept them, and the fact she felt he had to be prepared led him to speculation: that could only mean all the answers would stack together to form a staggering conclusion, something for which not only he, but all the people outside of the Skeins, was unprepared. Could it have something to do with the dreamweavers themselves, not just their political alliances?

That brought him to the question he'd been avoiding all along: why single him out as the recipient of her knowledge? Why groom him? Why him? The only response to that was one he found surprising, perhaps unlikely: Ela needed him because of the isolation he knew from his home planet, and from the very strangeness of his own species. It seemed easy for the xeno-body of sentience to accept nearly every form of life, from conscious plants and silica fibres to jellies and humanoids. But they reacted badly when confronted with a species which carried a spore which, while creating real advantages, also disfigured and transformed into something from the common sub-consciousness of nightmares. It was the extremity of Caliban strangeness Ela gambled would weigh in her favour.

Or was it?

His questions were left unasked as they journeyed that day. He respected Ela's wisdom. If she thought him unprepared, then he would wait. Everything about her told him that he would be fully enlightened when the time was right. And that brought him to another realization: he trusted her. No longer were his hunter instincts alerted when confronted with her. He looked to her as an ally. That meant there was a shift in alliance, in fundamental thinking. Maybe, just maybe, Calibans and dreamweavers had more in common than was apparent. Maybe there were similarities here not easily evident.

Too much speculation. Not enough evidence. He looked up to his surroundings, gaining his bearings in this weird and yet familiar landscape.

The countryside became more and more bizarre, as if the entire place had been created out of a child's dreams. To identify a species of tree was only possible by noting the shape of its leaves and the colour of its fruit, for two plants, equal in age and environment might differ in size as much as forty-five feet. Further on, he stopped and found no less than fourteen different flowers on one plant, different not just in colour and shape, but in pollination and reproduction methods.

That was when he analyzed the rocks they passed. What he discovered gave him no answers. There was everything here from igneous to sandstone rock, all jumbled into a collage without pattern or geological logic. Fault lines followed random ridges, often running in converging paths which, if real, would eventually create some of the most bizarre landforms known.

What made Tine consider that none of this was real was the lack of any wildlife. There were no creatures visiting flowers that obviously were not self-pollinating; neither were there any other creatures. There was no evidence of anything like nepanthaloids or other intelligent life-form.

Why?

For several hours now they had been climbing an escarpment. The scree proved easier than the cliff, and now, without any equipment, they faced an overhang that hung from the summit. Tine had his back pressed against the rock that felt warm and oily because of his hide.

Ela barely smiled when she said, "They told you you'd withdrawn." There was no question. Ela didn't need to question. She seemed to be aware of things beyond her world.

"They did," he answered, acknowledging the question in his own head beating to get out.

"And yet you're still exuding oils."

He growled and that startled him. "Why would IPCIB lie to me?"

"Maybe it wasn't IPCIB."

"Why must every conversation with you be a game of riddles?"

She shrugged. "It gets you thinking, doesn't it? Someone had to make you aware that you're still carrying the Setebian spore."

"So I'm carrying the spore. Why is it so important

to you that I be aware of that?" He didn't know whether to be ecstatic the spore might still be with him, leaving him in harmony with Setebos, or angry that he was still bound to a planet he thought he needed to abandon.

But was Setebos truly a planet to abandon? What was more binding? A planet where illusion was reality and reality simply a game, or a planet that forced aside attitudes about beauty and convention? Perhaps what was truly more horrific was how intelligent societies dealt with environment and each other.

He looked up at Ela, the way she studied him. She'd been laying a trail for him from the moment he arrived.

"Until you accept yourself," she said, "you'll never be able to accept what I am, and I need you to accept what I am."

She needed him? "Why?"

"I can't answer that yet." Her gaze swung to the overhang. "But I can give you something to think about."

For a few moments Tine speculated what that might be, hoping finally he would be given some hard evidence. His hope was in vain. Ela's *something* only raised more questions.

At first he thought some very thin cloud or fog rapidly approached, but it seemed too localized. And then it seemed too organized, almost intelligent in its motion. It collected near the precipice where they stood and spiralled upward in elegant arcs. All of it seemed black and white and grey, as if some invisible artist sketched with charcoal.

As he stared, open-mouthed, the thing infused with colour, like watercolour washes glazed over white paper, one over the other, warm to cool, light to dark, building layers that defied two-dimensionality.

When the thing stopped changing, Tine could feel the sharp edge of his canines cutting his chin, and was sure he looked foolish. He pulled his lips into place. His gaze swung to Ela who now stared down at him, smugness on her face.

"How?" He found himself incapable of completing the question. He wasn't even sure he wanted to know the answer.

Her long arm gestured toward the transparent staircase that had formed, the sleeve of her tattered gown fluttering. "We create our own realities."

"Don't spout theory! We don't create matter!"

She laughed. The sound of it was sensual, something born of sheer joy. "Maybe *you* don't, Tine my dear, but we do."

"We?" He stared at the whimsy.

"Dreamweavers. We create our own realities. Tell me what your reality is, Tine, and then maybe I can tell you of mine."

His gaze shifted back to her. "My reality?" He shrugged. "The here and now, what my senses report, what I can prove through intake of data."

"And what does your intake of data tell you now?"

"That there's a staircase here that isn't real."

Again she laughed. Tine thought of laughter ringing around his brood, the lack of laughter in the work-warrens. She stepped out onto the staircase, defying him to doubt her reality.

"What does your data tell you now?" she asked.

"That you're doing something that isn't logical or possible."

"We also create our own logic. There was a time we thought our worlds flat. Logic prevailed. Someone challenged logic. Now we think our worlds roughly spherical. What will we do when that logic is challenged?"

"But we have holographs to prove that fact! We see it with our own eyes in orbit."

"Do you? Or do you have something that confirms your reality?" She gestured to where she stood, her feet firmly supported by this unnatural creation. "I've created my own reality."

"You've woven this? That's what you're telling me? And because you've woven this that makes it real?"

"Wasn't my orgy?"

That was something Tine couldn't deny. Even before then Jabod had told him about impersonators that had been as real as the originals, and yet had faded away without any trace of real matter. Impersonators like the thread of the Gelt Ambassador.

"You're thinking about a dreamweaver's threads," she said carefully, as if she gauged his mood.

"Yes."

"And you're beginning to see that dreamweavers really do create not only their own reality, but the reality of those involved with them."

"Yes."

"Do you accept that?"

"I'm not sure if I accept it. But I am convinced of the fact's existence."

"Well, that's a beginning." She gestured to the stairs. "If you'll join me, I'll give you something else to think about."

He managed a grim facsimile of a smile. "That sounds like bribery."

She shrugged. "A form."

Tine knew he wouldn't refuse. He stepped gingerly beside her, one hoof at a time, testing, measuring, expecting at any moment to plummet down the scree, but when he didn't, he could only shake his head.

A long breath seemed to give him courage. "It's stable."

"It's real as long as I will it to be real." Her gaze flicked briefly to the horizon where Maxta lay. "I'll tell you something about dreamweavers you should know before we reach the summit, because I want you to realize how powerful we are in our own way, and that we wish you no harm."

"Continue," he said, cautiously. How did one deal with a species that could control reality?

"You wondered, no doubt, about the service, manufacturing, and labour industries in the city."

"I did. I wondered about the lack of people who pursued those trades, and I also wondered about the lack of children. There's no need to wonder now. I see how the children are used."

"Or abused."

"Yes."

"To address the first issue—dreamweaver children take care of the industries. They weave the waiters in the bistro you visited." She acknowledged his shock with a brief nod. "They weave the labourers. They spend all their childhoods slaves to their abilities. Most of them die—spontaneous combustion. Few of them reach adulthood and the Guild promise of apprenticing to an adept dreamweaver. And there's little any adult dreamweaver can do to help them. As I said—we create our own realities, and our children have been convinced their reality is thraldom to the Guild and those who elect the Guild." She smiled bitterly.

"Unfortunately, most alien children end up in the same situation. They die earlier than most, unable to provide themselves with food, heat, solace. We still haven't been able to convince any other species of our existence, and so they think weaving is a phenomenon spawned in childhood and nurtured in adversity."

"Then why am I convinced of your reality?"

"Because your reality is very much like ours. Our planets have made us kindred in our view of our realities. On Setebos, you accept illusion, ephemeral processes, the alien-ness of your species as compared to the rest of the solar system. Setebos claimed you twenty-four hours after birth when the spore became active in your mother's lactation and infected you."

"I don't see the parallel."

"Edain claims us just as Setebos claims you."

"A spore?"

"No spore. Over thousands of years we evolved to adapt to an atmosphere rich in hydrogen and indigent in basic food stuffs. Diamonds, gold, titanium, jade— these are of little use when you're starving. We now consume hydrogen."

This was more than he could accept. "But what was all that you told me about not eating anything yellow?"

"I was helping you to accept my reality. Would you have believed me if I told you that I don't eat as you eat?"

"No."

"You see how flawless was my reasoning."

"But was my eating a reality? Were the foodstuffs nourishing?"

"Were you hungry after you ate?"

"No."

"Then you were sated and nourished."

"But was it real? Was what I did and experienced real?"

"It was real. We can create matter, yes. Millions of years ago, no, we couldn't. It was a skill we acquired too late." Her fingers brushed against his warty cheek.

Tine shuddered. It unnerved him that this aloof alien could display such complete compassion. She used no standards. Nothing about Ela was predictable, and he desperately needed something by which he could guide himself. It was at that moment he realized she was gauging his mood by touching him.

"You're also an empath?"

She smiled. "When you want you can be very discerning, almost likeable. Yes, dreamweavers usually end up empaths. We have to feel what our characters feel in order to make them believable, and that has its side-effects."

He nodded to the summit. "What's up there?"

"The first loom."

"Then let's go."

She restrained his arm slightly. "Remember what I told you about realities when we get up there."

"Am I in for more surprises?"

"That depends on you."

TINE

RAIN **PRICKED** the escarpment, clouds scudding like shredded cloth across layered hills of grey and mauve. Tine remembered the last rain he'd seen, home on Setebos, the trees screaming in birth, the gorging which followed. He, Aganth and his brood. Doing what Calibans did. Aware of their place in the cycle of their world, comfortable with it, even to the point of ritual to mark their solemn stewardship. He wondered, at that point, whether he'd ever see Setebos again, whether he'd ever have the chance to seek Aganth's forgiveness, and if he did whether she'd consent to listen or kill him outright and feed him to their brood. It was her prerogative.

Either way he was aware death dogged him. He might never get off Edain alive.

He shifted his rump on the rock where he sat, one hoof crossed over the other knee. He'd been clawing out debris when he became aware of a flinty smell to the damp air, incongruous with the rain. Tine wondered if the hurried storm was part of some weaver's tapestry. If the weather was a tapestry, the weaver, Tine was sure, would be equal in power to Ela.

He let drop his leg, turned his attention to the immediate area. There was no use trying to call up communication with anyone off-planet through the conductive polish on his claws. The gold interface had long since chipped and broken away. And what would have been the point in that anyway? He wasn't sure of alignments and allies. And he hadn't been sure what to expect when he gained the summit of Ela's stairs, and it surely wasn't this thing with which he was now confronted. He knew he should be reacting, but reacting how? Should he be afraid of this thing? Should he be relieved he finally found some proof regarding the dreamweavers? Or should he feel nothing at all? Was this a normal situation?

Define normal.

It had been some hours now he'd watched this creature, and no closer now to any answers. The thing was difficult to identify at first. What with the inclement weather and drifting ribbons of fog, this person to whom Ela introduced him was virtually invisible.

It was for that reason he asked Ela where was this person. There had been no answer but for her laughter. Shortly after that a gaseous cloud, that reminded Tine of a miniature nebula, separated from the ambient fog and floated toward them. Tine bared his teeth: the thing seemed intelligent in its behaviour.

"You're telling me this is a dreamweaver," he managed to say after a few moments. There had

 CALIBAN

been no question in him. Ela was very clear in her introduction.

"Yes. This is Ethsa."

"You're asking me to believe your natural state is gaseous?"

"Yes."

"I can't do that!"

Her brow arched. "Why can't you? I accept your existence, and for me that's something equally bizarre."

Tine felt like yelling out, you win! But didn't. What Ela said made sense, strange as it might have been. It was fitting, somehow, that a species as misunderstood and unknown as dreamweavers should have a nebulous form.

His legs had felt weak. To save himself embarrassment, and to give himself a moment to think, he'd eased to the support of a rock, but both support and respite were denied. His rump met and melted through the white stone. When he hit something solid, pain shot up his back. He growled. Angry, he looked up at Ela and her cloudy companion. His anger shifted to shock, then curiosity. He stared up through what seemed to be solid stone, and yet he was no more trapped than he was in the air.

"I don't understand," he'd managed to stammer, Ela's laughter ringing round him. "I touched this rock when we first came up here and it felt solid enough."

She offered him a hand, those elongated eyes crinkling with humour. "Ethsa is very old, Tine, and age has made it tremulous when weaving realities. Not long now and Ethsa will leave Edain for another home." Tine was on his feet. She gestured to the sky. "Out there."

Since then he'd been thinking. He could feel questions on his tongue, each as immediate as the next.

Now, finally he felt able to have a meaningful conversation. He rubbed the warts on his head.

"You said Ethsa would be ready for another home out there. What do you mean *out there?*"

"Space...to the nebula, where other dreamweavers go."

He managed a toothy smile. "This isn't going to be easy."

"I know," she answered softly. "But ask away, because you're our only link to the UOoP, and we must be heard."

Tine bobbed his head in a nod. The rain cooled his confusion.

"You're telling me this cloud is a dreamweaver," he said at length.

"Yes."

"And that his name is Ethsa."

"Its name, yes, is Ethsa. You can't think in terms of gender with us, Tine. We have none. We aren't at all analogous with anything yet discovered."

"You're trying to tell me that I mated with an it? I know female flesh when I touch it."

"That's me. Not Ethsa."

"So you're not a dreamweaver?"

"Of course I am."

"This isn't making sense."

"I'm not as mature as Ethsa. I haven't evolved to that state yet.

"And when you do?"

"I'll have accumulated enough mass that I'll be like Ethsa."

"Is that what happened when Moishen combusted, when that child died?"

"I absorbed their masses, yes. It's dangerous."

"Why?"

"What happens when a nebula's mass reaches that critical state under pressure of gravity?"

"A star." He turned his attention away, looked out to a landscape he wasn't even sure was real.

A star?

Was it possible these creatures were the beginning of stars? It was something he felt incapable of understanding. Not yet. Little bits and little bits. That's how information should be absorbed, each morsel digested, the flavour of it recognizable, and then on to the next. He dealt with a question he felt better able to absorb.

"Why is Ethsa having difficulty weaving realities?"

"Because its molecular state is reaching the culmination of another stage. It has become difficult for Ethsa to remain in this reality, and for that reason its loom is here, close to the borderlands. The fact Ethsa's tapestries are now erratic has become one of our best defences against the Guild."

"What will Ethsa do in space?" Tine wasn't even sure he wanted to hear an answer to that question, but he knew it had to be asked.

"At first Ethsa will be a part of the nebula. The

nebula will evolve, and then there will be another metamorphosis, and another, and another. Ethsa will go through many more forms, perhaps even become part of one of your descendants...eventually.”

“This is all a little difficult to comprehend, Ela.”

“Why? You come from a people who deal with metamorphosis.”

“I may come from a people who deal with metamorphosis, but none of that could prepare me for this.”

“You must try. There’s so much at stake.”

“Like what?”

“Like the future of the Guild, of the people who work and live in the domes, of the children in the work-warrens, of the very fabric of the dreamweavers’ existence.”

“Is there jeopardy here?” He could see how there might, and Ela’s nod confirmed his suspicion.

“How?” he asked, so lowly he could barely hear himself. “How is there jeopardy?”

“We can’t live with other species,” she answered, as if she’d been stating a fact of her health. “Not because we don’t want to, but because of species incompatibility. We’re a danger.”

“Am I in danger?”

“Not yet...but eventually, yes.”

“You’re contradicting yourself, Ela. You told me the important hostages were safe.”

“And they are. For the moment.”

Another voice echoed around him. “We aren’t wilfully jeopardizing either you or anyone else. We only need to be heard so that you will understand what we are, and leave us."

Tine tried hard not to show his shock. It hadn't occurred to him the cloud would be capable of auditory communication. The sharp edge of the rain helped keep his dignity. Distantly, he wondered of what the rain consisted. It couldn't be simple water, a bonding of two hydrogen atoms to one oxygen, not with this much hydrogen and helium around. Or could it? Was this rain real? He asked that.

Ela shook her head slowly.

He thought about that, then: "Ethsa's weaving."

She nodded.

"Ethsa can weave while talking to me, without incandescence." Tine stated a fact out loud. He needed no confirmation from Ela.

"Ethsa has sufficient mass to do that."

Tine's scrutiny now took hold of the gaseous dreamweaver. "A sufficient mass," he said, thinking of the way Ela sometimes glowed when weaving, thinking of how she had been utterly brilliant when he'd found her combusting. "A sufficient mass," he said again. His gaze shot up to Ela. "Hydrogen? Sufficient mass to cause incandescence?" He jumped to his feet. "Impossible! You haven't enough mass to incandesce! Besides, stars aren't sentient!"

"Not all stars are sentient, Tine," Ethsa echoed around him. "But the smaller ones, yes, the ones which usually twin with a larger star, and those which are yellows, yes."

"It's not as if each of us, individually, become stars," Ela said. "We try not to allow the metamorphosis

to progress that far. It's..." her face twisted, "...
dangerous."

He felt utterly ridiculous when he asked, "Why?"

"It takes many of us to achieve star state. The
sacrifice is too great."

"What do the others become?"

"We metamorphose slowly," Ethsa said, its voice
rumbling like a disembodied giant, "so that star state
doesn't have an opportunity to attract others."

"But what do you become?" he pressed.

"I'm not sure you're prepared for this, Tine," Ela
said.

"Ready or not, I have to know!" he roared,
frustrated and unnerved. He wanted urgently to
be back on Setebos with Aganth and his brood,
immersing himself in the rituals that would now
bring him comfort and meaning. There, everything
had its place. There was order. There was purpose.
And now he had none of these. The very fabric of his
beliefs was being challenged by some of the most
preposterous claims he'd ever heard.

Ela closed her eyes, almost as if she meditated on
an answer. Presently, she said, "We become part of a
nebula, then dark matter."

"Right," he growled. "And two and two equals ten.
Get serious, Ela. I'm not an idiot!"

Ela nodded, but Tine knew it wasn't in
acknowledgement of anything he'd said, or even of
his existence. When Ethsa moved toward him he
knew Ela had given some form of permission to the
cloud.

He didn't have an opportunity to protest. Ethsa

engulfed him as completely as a second skin. The sensations weren't unpleasant, rather they were like being rocked in the arms of a being that had achieved a god-like state. There was no ugliness here. Neither was there beauty. Illusion and reality blurred the lines of distinction. To be a dreamweaver was to be an existence where anything was possible, an existence in which elements were created in the way an alchemist tried to conjure gold from lead. To be a dreamweaver was to be a creator of matter. An elemental.

When Ethsa released him, Tine could only stare out across the Skeins. There was no need to tell Ela he was prepared for anything he might yet face.

Lack of understanding of a thing isn't justification for fear or ridicule. And yet fear and ridicule the dreamweavers you will. That's a predictable reaction. They know that. What they're asking of you is to overcome your fear. Fear is the result of lack of facts. Dreamweavers will provide you with all the facts you require. What they're asking of you is to override your ridicule. Ridicule is the result of ignorance. With the facts they will provide, you will no longer be ignorant.

THE EDAIN TRIAL, JURY ADDRESS FROM THE
DREAMWEAVER COMMISSIONER TINE.

FOR DAYS after he met Ethsa, Tine travelled deeper and deeper into the southern latitudes with Ela, where the landscape changed into something he'd come to call an airscape. He might even have walked through scores of dreamweavers by now. There was no way of knowing. Not after meeting Ethsa. What could alert him to a dreamweaver? There were no familiar standards. No signposts. No triggers. This was an existence in a universe of unknowns.

How he even managed to walk through the vaporous stuff in this region eluded him, but by now he'd grown beyond question. Questions served no purpose. Questions were born out of the references from his own life. Nothing of his own life was here in this land of illusion. It was easier to accept what he saw. Leave the questions for something else.

What he saw was a planet more cloud than land mass, cloud that logically should have asphyxiated him long ago. Yet he still breathed the vapour. He still lived. His body still was nourished by what filled his heart-lung. And beneath his hooves there was solid ground. He could feel it. Yet there were all these swirling, eddying clouds, and no moisture on his skin. None of it fit itself into logic. Logic would not prevail.

More weaving?

If it was more weaving, he couldn't tell. Ela's power as a dreamweaver amplified the farther they delved into the Skeins, power that was subtle, insidious, unidentifiable. For all he knew he walked through a tapestry of her own making. He thought of the rock he'd fallen through in Ethsa's loom. It had been so real one moment. The next it was nothing more than a mirage. Would he find himself adrift in space when Ela chose? Would he awaken aboard the IPCIB liner, shaking his head against dreams? Was any of this real? What was reality?

Again, there were no answers. There were only the moors of clouds rolling endless on.

Periodically, as they walked, the clouds parted, revealing ground of grey-pink he couldn't be sure was solid or gaseous. All of this was adorned with columns that shifted direction and colour without pattern or reason. Had he not been so afraid, he'd have taken delight in this bizarre place he visited. He kept remembering what Ela told him when he met Ethsa: dreamweavers were not only the stuff of stars, but dark matter itself. That wasn't exactly what she'd said, but the intent was the same. There was the possibility of creation and destruction all around them. They were dangerous to be with. Even he was in danger, here, in this place of dreams.

What disturbed him most was the silence. Long ago the wind harps ceased their moaning, left in the twisted trees of the borderlands. More than the lack of any wildlife, he missed the harps. They had filled the ominous silence that now swallowed him. Quiet. Utterly quiet. The quiet threatened to completely absorb him it was so huge. He was aware his mouth hung open, a question ready to spill toward Ela. No. No questions now. There was only so much he could assimilate.

So he sang to fill the silence, letting his scratchy voice make a place for him. He sang a Caliban walking song, rhythmic, melodious, counterpointed with the way his people had of making clicks and whistles. It was the walking song he'd sung when the first born of his brood passed between Aganth's legs, a song to tell the land of their fecundity.

Ela seemed not to mind. She only smiled and kept to a course that would take them into the heart of the churning columns of vapour. Not long after that his stomach churned, pushing his hunger to the point of urgency. He made no comment, and only accepted the things she pulled out of the air for him to eat. It was something he had come to understand about her—she did care for him in her own way. She would see that he came to no harm. And so a trust of sorts grew between them.

They travelled in this manner for another three

days—Tine filling the walking hours with songs from his homeworld, Ela walking to the rhythms he introduced to her world of illusion. The enormity of his surroundings left him dwarfed, a brown wart in a world of gossamer. As the sun and moons turned he grew less and less uncomfortable. There was a place in every world for a wart. It was what made life interesting. Ela taught him that much.

They stopped early that evening, as was their custom, more to allow him an opportunity to settle before the long night of weaving, than to give any respite to Ela. Before darkness completely claimed the land, Tine had already lowered himself into the vapour at his feet, his skin sensitive to the hard surface concealed by the cloud. As had occurred during their previous camps, he expected no conversation. Ela granted little in that direction. Tonight, he was sure, would be no different.

"Tell me about your homeworld, Tine."

He flinched, looking to where she sat cross-legged, cloaked in a robe of tatters that did little to conceal or protect. The look on her face was enough to prod him. He would deny nothing to her with such pain evident.

"What about it? You seem to know already a great deal about Setebos."

"Are you like the humanoids of the Guild? Do you take mates, strive for success, achievements, advancements?"

"I'd like to think we aren't like the Guild members. We live according to what Setebos dictates."

"You take no mates?"

"One only."

"You're monogamous?"

He nodded.

She smiled. "The Guild would find that confining."

"I find the Guild confining."

"You have a mate?"

There was an ache he couldn't name inside him when he confirmed her question. Silence then. Finally, he added, "Aganth. Her name's Aganth. You've woven her for me." He remembered how he'd condemned Aganth before he left.

Such cruelty. For what? To wound her for what he wouldn't acknowledge himself?

Only now he realized he'd looked into the face of paradise here and found only evil. There had been nothing but paradise with Aganth.

"But we're divorced," he added. "That's all in the past." He slid down into the cloud and let the vapour conceal his anguish. The threads Ela spun bothered him not at all that night. It was a tapestry of quietude, of fragrant fires and savoury meals, of family and glowing looks. It was a tapestry she wove to rock him into peace.

The next day, when they again took up their journey, nothing was mentioned about their conversation the previous night. Tine was grateful for that. He did, however, sing once more, again the simple songs of his homeworld. Today Ela hummed in harmony.

The airscape made another gradual change as they went, now to places where the clouds parted entirely and revealed rock, pink, pale, like the granite that formed the foothills of his home. There was nothing insubstantial about this. This was as real and demanding as his home. For a moment he wondered what season it was on that planet called Setebos, what ritual had taken his brood into another cycle. He paused, staring at the pink rock at his feet, Aganth overwhelming his sensations. They had parted with such harsh words. It was not the way of Calibans. Fierce they might be in matters of survival. But tenderness between mates was the way of things, the way things should be. It was a mark of trust. *I am vulnerable before you. Treat that with care.*

Ela's hand on his shoulder brought his attention back up. Question there. Her mouth shut the sound out. But he would answer. He owed her that much.

"I miss my home."

Her smile was all the response he needed. He knew that she, more than anyone, would understand what he meant. Once more he pushed his legs into action, pleased that at least his hooves now made some sound.

There will be pressure on many of you to weight your decision in favour of the Edain Guild. That's understandable. It's understandable because we, all of us, are only mortal. Who wouldn't be seduced by the promise of wealth, by the opportunity to have our children trained by some of the best artists and artisans in the UOoP? I'm telling you this is a false dream. Edain was proof of that. We need only look at the fate of dreamweaver children to know the lure you've been offered holds nothing but purgatory. Paradise isn't always what it seems.

THE EDAIN TRIAL, JURY ADDRESS FROM THE
DREAMWEAVER COMMISSIONER TINE.

IT WAS of children Tine thought throughout the next day. Their laughter and their tears filled his world. It was impossible for him to conceive of any future without them. Dreamweaver children. His own children. It made little difference. What would any of them be without the children? There would be no hope. There would be no tomorrow. There would be no eternity.

Gone. All gone with the children.

By the time they reached a valley of stone, he'd sharpened his teeth on plans. He'd say nothing of them now. Now wasn't the right moment, as it was apparent they approached their destination, the loom where the hostages were held. He could tell they approached because of Ela's agitation, the way she'd toss him glances fraught with worry, the way her own form melted and wavered and reformed.

By the time they entered a valley swathed in cloud, his concern for her grew. There was nothing of the aloof, cool dreamweaver about her now. There was only this nervous creature. Her gaze darted, her hands flexing at her sides as if warding off some attack.

Tine's attention swung back to the valley. There were still the ubiquitous clouds, although these were now confined to a ring around the bowl. The open air revealed smooth pink granite, pools of liquid about which Tine could only speculate. A shelter of pink rock had been constructed, crudely, only to meet the requirements of shelter and privacy, and around this was gathered an assortment of people. Jabod was among them. It wasn't hard for Tine to identify that tall, dark man, the way he moved as if all of one movement, fluid, sinuous.

He remembered feeling clownish against him. Strange that he felt no such discomfort now. Perhaps Edain had affected him in more ways than he realized. Perhaps it was the knowledge he was still in symbiosis with Setebos, or perhaps he'd finally come to accept what he was, Caliban, a hunter, a species attuned to his environment and living within it. Perhaps it was a little of all of these. At the moment all he knew was he'd been deceived by a man he'd admired for years. Jabod told him the spore would die. It hadn't. What had occurred was an elaborate deception, cost no object, whether material or trust.

His anger smouldered, hidden, buried. Lies were something for which even Caliban children had been known to kill.

His gaze flicked up to the lip of the valley where trails of vapour hung like mauve-coloured gauze, pale, fragile in the last embers of sunset. Dreamweavers. The clouds were dreamsweavers. He was sure of it. This was what Ethsa had looked like. The set of Ela's face confirmed this.

"Why mature weavers?" he asked. "Why take such a risk?"

She shuddered. "Only mature weavers are capable of providing our guests' needs."

She had no need to explain just how aware the weavers were of the dangers here. Danger rang from every word, creased her face, echoed around those who watched from the lip of the valley. To have this many mature weavers gathered in one place was to risk an accretion of mass which would in turn risk combustion. The only way to prevent that was to refrain from weaving. And that was something from which no dreamweaver could refrain for too long. To weave was to them as breathing was to his kind. He'd seen what that need had done to Ela throughout their many nights together. There had been nothing she could do to prevent it.

It was then the silence of the dreamweavers hit him. There was conversation percolating from the hostages, movement. But from the dreamweavers there was nothing. None of them moved, nor spoke, nor made any movement that required an expenditure of energy. Tine lifted his gaze to Ela. She nodded.

"It's that serious, Tine. Any miscalculation could catalyze a sequence of events that would be catastrophic. Even to move would be unconscionable." She gestured to the hostages who by now had turned toward their visitors, their faces full of question in the light of the evening fire. "I'll leave you with our guests. Whatever you can devise to save us is now your responsibility."

"You aren't going to help?"

She shook her head. "My reality doesn't encompass that. I've done all I may."

"But you did such a good job convincing me."

"You convinced yourself. Setebos did that to you. You were prepared for the kinds of things I've shown you. They? They understand nothing of what I am. Of what we are."

"But just a demonstration—"

"With other dreamweavers around?" She shook her head.

"Then let's take them elsewhere."

"It would make little difference. You see, they've all seen dreamweavers spin yarns, weave tapestries. They have a mindset. That's their reality. Nothing I demonstrated would be anything but a master writer incarnating a story."

"What makes you think I'll do any better?"

"Because you also know of reality. At the moment they only know of illusion." She touched his warty arm. "The rest is up to you, Caliban."

He flinched. The last time she'd called him that had

been after the nightmare of the orgy. He thought it had been a condemnation. Now he saw it for what it was. She merely identified his reality. He was Caliban—a creature bound by ritual and symbiosis with a planet that dictated his every move, just as Edain dictated who and what Ela would be. She had made a statement of kindred spirits. In his reality he might be able to save the dreamweavers. Might.

She drifted off to join the others at the summit. They seemed so ghostly now that night crept around them, some insubstantial.

Tine shouldered the weight of his task and crossed to Jabod. Words fired between the hostages, some hostile, others surprised, others with nothing but question. Jabod set off in a sprint toward Tine, his teeth white in his face. For just a moment he leaned toward Tine, his arms open, then he halted, frowned, straightened. Tine did nothing to encourage Jabod to complete the embrace. He simply stood there, staring, waiting to see what direction Jabod would take.

"So she's taken you hostage also," the Commissioner said, nodding to where Ela had gone.

Tine kept his voice level, his gaze steady. "Not quite."

Jabod retreated a step. Tine felt his violence. It shrieked like an alarm around him.

Treason! Traitor! How could you do this, Tine?

"It's all right, Commissioner. I'm still serving my mission."

Jabod's violence shifted, now to caution, the reserve of the Commissioner. He hissed a warning through his teeth, indicating the others. They weren't alone.

"They need to hear everything I'm about to tell you," Tine said. "The time for secrecy is over."

Jabod blanched. "You're not going to discuss—"

"Everything. Why I was sent here, their plot, circumstances about which they know nothing and must now know everything."

Tine passed his gaze over the others—the Gelt Ambassador, a young woman who was an Active he assumed was Jabod's daughter, a representative like Master Tylan from Forest, others as varied as the people he'd seen on the streets of Maxta. There were VIPs here from every planet in the UOoP, from every organization, every sphere of influence. Ela had done her job well. He wondered if the Guild realized how well.

The Gelt shouldered his way forward, pompous, ridiculous in his slashed costume that had once been so elaborate. Tine almost laughed aloud with the absurdity of it.

"Secrecy about what?" the Gelt demanded.

"In due time," Tine answered.

The Gelt's mouth hung open, snapped shut. He still sputtered indignation when Jabod waved him to silence. One stroke of the hand. That's all it took. It gave Tine an indication of how much respect Jabod carried among these people. Convince Jabod and he might be able to convince the rest.

Whispers hissed around the gathering. Tine knew his task wouldn't be easy. None of them were prepared for the political brouhaha that would ensue, but he would speak until he had convinced them all of the reality of dreamweavers, of the necessity to abandon Edain…and then he would deal with Jabod.

He squatted where he stood. To his surprise the others eased to the ground around him, in pockets, too plain in their alliances, but plainly acquiescent for the moment to his authority. He speculated just what Setebos would gain if it were to open to interplanetary immigration. Very little, judging from the avarice on their faces. He remembered Ela's warning: *If you're smart you'll lobby to keep the Guild out.*

"What's this all about?" Jabod asked.

It was all Tine could do to keep his claws sheathed, to prevent himself from letting outrage shout from every wart. "The UOoP has to abandon Edain."

There was no other way to say it, and the effect of that statement was all too predictable. The potentates bubbled with outrage, questions ringing round his head. He raised his hand against their words.

"There are intelligent life-forms on Edain that are incompatible with alien life-forms," he said, "A people who—"

"There were extensive studies," the Gelt Ambassador said. "I know. I financed most of them."

"Studies or not—"

"I know what came back on those reports! There were no intelligent life-forms!"

"No intelligence for which you could monitor." Tine shook his head. "Hasn't it occurred to you there might very well be intelligence that would be unidentifiable to your scans, your tests?" His omission of Setebos from their group was glaring to him. None of them caught it. Setebos was of no concern to them—a backwater planet with a backward people.

"That's preposterous!" another hostage sputtered.

"Look at how long it took the UOoP to find out about Calibans."

That stifled their protests. He'd need that moment. "The native Edains are an intelligence we've come to know as dreamweavers, a people capable of creating matter, of creating realities—"

"You're not feeling well," Jabod said. "The journey here—"

"I'm fine. Just look around you and then tell me that we're not in the southern latitudes. Look at the passage of the sun, how high it rises, where it sets—if you remember how to judge those kinds of things. Then tell me this place is uninhabitable just as all the research and costly observations say." He watched Jabod's face twist with understanding. "Remember the way it was with Setebos. You didn't think we Calibans were worth considering as intelligent because we didn't live according to your rules—no architecture, no agriculture as you know it, no sociological groups outside of the breeding clans. It wasn't until some scientists dared the spore that the UOoP realized we are very much intelligent, very much worth bothering about." He grinned. "Of course, the spore helped convince you that we were worth leaving alone, that our planet had nothing you'd want, unlike Edain."

"But the planet was without any life-forms," Jabod said. "It was a mineral-rich, lifeless planet."

"Everything we know about Edain has been what the dreamweavers have allowed us to know."

"That's preposterous."

"Is it? Consider how well Ela up there," and he gestured in her direction, "convinced us all that her threads were the people she'd taken hostage. We had no idea how extensive her deception had been, until now."

"Okay," another hostage said, "say the dreamweavers are an intelligent life-form. Why make us think the south is inhospitable?"

"Because they couldn't risk having aliens inhabit this area. Dreamweavers are a danger to be with."

"Nonsense," Jabod said. "In every city there are dreamweavers living compatibly with other species. There are even dreamweavers on the planets in the UOoP."

"It may seem like compatibility to us, here, on Edain, but for them it's dangerous, as it will become to us if we don't leave them alone."

"Why?'

"Because they're dark matter."

An explosion of derisive laughter tore through the gathering. He'd expected no less. His reaction had been much the same.

As if he might find support in her, he let his gaze drift up the bowl to Ela. Against the black sky she was no more than a silhouette, black on black, utterly still. Just the shape of her filled him with awe. She was so beyond anything he could hope to understand, and yet he'd shared countless days with her, days that allowed him an acute understanding of her, days that seemed more like years. She was this creature of legend. Untouchable. Peerless. Terrible in her mystery. A dreamweaver.

She smiled on him. He realized he could see her smile. Alarm slammed through him. Oil slicked his skin. If he could see Ela smile that meant there was light. Frantic, he jumped to his feet, spun around, desperate to find out which dreamweaver wove.

There. Directly across the bowl from Ela. The glow was unmistakable even from a nebulous form. It was that pale, yellow glow that accompanied the burn-off effect of hydrogen in combustion. Heat accompanied that glow this time, heat that had never been evident when Ela wove. Was it because of the mature state of this dreamweaver? Was it actually burning like a tiny star?

He wheeled back to Ela. A few of the other dreamweavers drifted away like evaporating clouds. He felt frenetic against their torpidity.

"Do something!" he yelled at her. "Stop it from weaving!"

Her eyes were wide with terror.

Too late. He knew it was too late. Why else were the other dreamweavers fleeing?

A wail grew out of nowhere, clawing at his skin. He screamed into the sound, afraid, ready to bolt at any moment but held his ground. He wheeled back around. The dreamweaver had completely combusted, just like a tiny star. It took flight, unwillingly, dragged across the bowl of the valley toward Ela.

Mass, he remembered. It had to do with mass.

Ela!

"No!" he roared, pivoting once more to face that tall, foreign woman. As he watched, riveted, the ball of fire swallowed Ela, or rather Ela swallowed fire. One more dreamweaver disappeared into her body before the damage ended. All the others fled. Only Ela remained, her face twisting with a pain he couldn't identify.

Shaken, he confronted the hostages who were open-mouthed, rigid with horror.

"That's what happens if we stay," he said. He'd asked Ela for a demonstration. This was more than eloquent.

A few invectives flew among them.

He could hear Jabod swallow, say, "I don't understand."

"They're dark matter. The more pressure we put on them, the more they integrate and create individuals with greater mass. All of you know what happens when a protostar gains enough mass under gravitational force."

"It becomes a star," Jabod said.

Tine nodded. He left them to swim in their stew of discovery. Danger or not, he made his way to Ela, cradling her fears in the leather of his arms, as she had once cradled him.

THE EDAIN TRIAL, JURY ADDRESS FROM THE
DREAMWEAVER COMMISSIONER TINE.

NOTHING MORE was said between Tine and the hostages for several days. They avoided him as if he were a pariah, to the point they even shunned him during meals. He ate at the lip of the valley on things Ela wove for him, watching, always studying.

Later, when study wasn't enough, Tine occupied himself building a dry waterfall out of striated rocks he found in his wanderings, letting the exertion of carrying them exhaust his body, but more, exhaust his mind. Ela only watched, from a distance, periodically creating a rock of which Tine would think. He knew she did this for him. He did nothing to stop that small tapestry. It was, at least, something they could share—this earth-bound wart and this star-blown cloud—he building the illusion of a waterfall out of rock, she building an illusion of rock out of air.

After that first night Ela had grown more and more distant. One conversation with her had given him adequate reason to agree with her isolation. Inadvertently he'd touched her arm. It had been an act of compassion. At least, he thought he'd touched her arm. His fingers had passed right through her. Their conversation had been about grim statistics, about the facts around dreamweavers. That occurrence did everything to cement the information he'd received. Ela was heading for that transition all dreamweavers avoided. It would continue if circumstances didn't change. She had gained too much mass.

It was for that reason he now built a dry waterfall. This was something tangible, something real, real because he did it. Not even Ela was tangible anymore. Try as he might he couldn't envision what her life might be like if she achieved star-state all on her own. Everything about Edain would slip through his fingers. None of it was constant enough to last the day. It surprised him this should bother him. This ephemeral process was something with which he was accustomed. Setebos was like this. But here, it seemed so hard to accept.

He paused now, letting his breathing even out, his rump against the hard stone. That last boulder had been almost more than he could move. But he'd placed it, just as he wanted.

Jabod came upon him from behind. Tine flinched. Hunter stalking hunter. Ancient Masai and ancient Caliban.

"There's no need for stealth, Jabod."

Tine could almost feel the Commissioner flinch, straighten.

"A little caution is always prudent," Jabod answered, crossing his arms, his dark eyes intent as he watched Tine.

"What do you want?"

"Some answers."

Tine let his gaze flick to Ela who stood at a little distance, back to Jabod. He realized he'd become a part of the unknown, the opposing camp. That would unsettle the Commissioner. "Ask."

"What happened the other night?"

"An accretion of matter."

"You told me that. What really happened?"

"An accretion of matter."

"He speaks the truth," Ela said, keeping her distance.

Jabod glared at her. "I want some proof."

"You're the one who spouted proof to me," Tine said. "What was all that about aberrations in the behaviour of certain potentates, in your daughter?"

"Just that. Aberrations. None of that proves what you're saying about protostars and dark matter."

"You're just unwilling to accept it."

"Agreed," Ela said. "It does nothing to prove we're protostars." She waved to the huddle of hostages. "For every one of them there has been a thread created, a duplicate I have woven and directed. Did you ever doubt their reality while they were active? Was there any reason to doubt? No. Only when a few dissolved did doubt come into question, your aberrations, as you say. They dissolved only because I was under pressure, incapable of maintaining so broad a tapestry. That's where your deaths came from. That's what brought us Tine."

"Why bother?" Jabod asked. "Why bother to go to such an elaborate ruse?"

"For myself there were two purposes. Foremost,

to force the Edain Guild to look to me for their base of power. They would have no reason to suspect me, then, of being the rebel leader."

"The rebels are—"

"Dreamweavers. Rebels are what the Guild chooses to call us. There are a few dreamweavers who have managed to mature in the domed settlements." Her gaze softened when she turned to Tine. "Moishen was one of them." Tine nodded. She gave her attention back to Jabod. "Together, we're trying to convince the Guild of dreamweaver existence through our tapestries, but all the Guild sees are talented humanoids who are threatening Guild authority, and they want that authority extended throughout the UOoP."

"And the Guild's purpose for replacing these hostages with their own people?"

"That would be their way of gaining power. The threads I'd weave would exist as I've directed, puppets."

"So you're working to cross-purposes."

"In a way, yes." She smiled. "It's not as easy for us, as it is for you, to make embodied intelligence recognize our existence. We are a people who create realities out of illusion. I made myself real to the Guild, as a child, desperate to do something to save our kind. Unlike so many dreamweaver children, I stole my way into Maxta, created a reality that made the Guild think I'd always been a part of the apprenticeship program, and rose quickly to the rank of Master Dreamweaver. I've suffered through the work-warrens. I am what I have made them think I am. They had no way of suspecting that I was a native, a rebel child." She gestured to the airscape around them. "That I was part of all this."

Now Tine understood why Ela's home in Maxta had been a cloud formation. It was a way of reminding herself of her reality. Her weaving might have become so adept she'd come to believe the tapestry she wove for the Guild and have forgotten, like so many others, just what she was.

He remembered Moishen's yarn—art controlling the artist. Perhaps the tapestry had been a warning not only to the Guild, but to the dreamweavers who had been present: don't weave so well that you become a thread.

"What about other dreamweaver children?" Jabod asked.

Tine's gaze swung back up. "They're held in slavery, in work-warrens. The Guild may use the euphemistic term of apprenticeship, but it's still nothing more than slavery, slavery of the worst kind."

"I've heard nothing about these work-warrens."

"They're very much a reality. Children, both dreamweaver and alien, are tested for high psi ratings and taken into the Guild apprenticeship program. The adults are all so involved in the industry of art and the political and social statements, let alone power, they could gain, that they've no time for the survival and service industries. The children do all that. The dreamweaver children do all that.

"Death rate in the program is ninety percent. Those who survive are all dreamweavers, natives, caught in a reality of their own making. These children need to weave, to spin tapestries, and it's that need, that reality, that traps them."

"The survival rate with them?"

"Twelve percent. Those who die, do so from spontaneous combustion and are absorbed by another dreamweaver with greater mass. That creates a critical situation. The dreamweavers who survive the apprenticeship program have achieved more mass than is safe for the natives in the Skeins. It's for that reason Ela's made those dreamweavers Guild representatives throughout the UOoP. Survival."

Jabod shook his head. "What causes a normal death?"

"There is no normal death for us," Ela replied. "We simply are, evolving from state to state. We're born of flesh. We evolve to small pockets of hydrogen gas, and from there amass with the nebula in which this star and planet have been created. Eventually the nebula will create another star. Both stars will eventually create elements until they can create no more, and from there we release the beginnings of more dreamweavers—dark matter."

"Dark matter has no mass. It has no energy. It can't create a life."

"Not a life as you know it. The spaces and delineations you give your world don't apply to us. We pass through those spaces."

"You're lying!" Jabod growled.

Tine almost roared out of frustration. Not yet. Not now. Now's not the right moment. But the hunter was upon him. He could do little to stop himself.

"Lying's more your style."

Jabod glared at him. "What's that supposed to mean?"

"You told me the spore would die, that I'd be injected with a synthetic that would allow me to return to Setebos." His claws unsheathed. "The spore's still active."

Jabod's mouth hung open.

"Deny it."

"I...I—"

"Deny it."

"They told me you'd withdraw! Everything I read confirmed that."

Now!

Tine tensed for the kill. Ela's voice brought him back. "He's telling the truth."

Tine eased, his body trembling with adrenalin.

"It's the truth!!" Jabod gasped. "I thought you'd withdrawn."

Tine could find nothing to say for a moment. Adrenaline screamed through his system, making his hands shake, his knees tremble. He could feel oil slick on his skin. The immensity of the Guild's deception staggered him. If Jabod really hadn't known Tine would remain with the spore, that could only mean Luther from IPCIB was involved. Who else knew about sending in Tine?

As always, he looked to Ela. "You knew?"

She nodded.

"Then why not tell me?"

"Realities are something each existence must discover for themselves."

The weight of knowledge turned again. This tapestry was of Ela's making. "How big is this plot that they'd dupe the Commissioner of IPCIB?"

Ela answered, "Enormous."

It should be comforting for you to know that we are watched and nurtured by billions of brilliant beings.

THE EDAIN TRIAL, JURY ADDRESS FROM THE
DREAMWEAVER COMMISSIONER TINE

YOU CAN'T run from what you are.

Tine shivered. Despite all of Aganth's warnings that was exactly what he'd tried to do. And now the running would stop.

His lifted his gaze from his hooves to the pastel clouds around him. Dawn defined the airscape—ragged edges of vapour, sharp edges of rock. Mist dampened his skin. He blinked at the pleasure of it, letting the warm wind ease his tension, letting the silences of Edain echo through him. There was only Aganth at his core, Aganth with whom he'd shared all the rituals that defined his life and his existence. Aganth to whom he would return. If she would have him. If she didn't kill him first.

There were tears on his face. He knew this. He did nothing to hide them. It mattered little if someone saw that he wept. He was Caliban. If a person chose to misinterpret what he did, so be it. These tears were in acknowledgement of a life past, and hope for a life in the future.

Something brushed his arm. His gaze shot up. Ela.

She stood there like a ghost, almost nebulous, thin, that thing in her eyes screaming. The smile on her face denied it all—compassionate, warm, willing to take on his worries.

"What is it, Tine?"

He inhaled sharply, knowing his body craved oxygen in quantities Edain couldn't afford. "I've been thinking about my home."

She only nodded.

"Where is your home, Ela?"

That seemed to unbalance her. Her smile evaporated, like mist in morning sun. She shrugged. "Here."

He gestured to the airscape. "All this? This is what you call home? This is your loom?"

She nodded.

"No mate with whom you share ritual? No shelter from the elements, from predators?"

"From what would I shelter myself? There is nothing that preys upon us. I am elemental. I can't shelter myself from myself. As for mate—that's a tapestry better left unwoven."

He accepted that, turning his attention back to the ever-changing vista. "How is it that the children end up in the work-warrens?"

"There's a patrol once a month."

"A patrol?"

"The Guild has the dreamweaver children in the work-warrens spin threads that are patrol officers, and they, in turn, go outside the domes on foot, luring wandering dreamweaver children from the borderlands into the city."

"Why would the children in the work-warrens do that?"

"I told you before—they're convinced the way they live is their reality. It's what must be."

"So what happened to you?"

She smiled. "I spent my early days wandering with natural dreamweavers who knew the tragedy of the cities. I wanted to be taken into Maxta, for the then nascent rebellion, to give us a chance."

"What would happen if the dreamweaver children were released back to the Skeins?"

"There would be less likelihood of a star occurring."

"And if things remain as they are?"

"A star is inevitable."

"What kind of a star?"

"I'm not sure. Usually we evolve into small yellows, as I told you before, the kind of stars that cause life on their orbiting planets. But there have been occasions...."

"Of?"

"Black stars."

The image filled him with foreboding. All he could remember was the terrifying feeling he'd had when coupled with Ela, a feeling of being sucked into another existence.

"If that didn't happen? Is there another possibility if the children aren't released?"

"We'd been drawn simultaneously by the existing star. That would cause an equally dangerous situation."

"How so?"

"If the existing star were to suddenly gain that much mass, it would cause a catastrophic explosion. Anything could happen from a red giant to a supernova and the creation of a neutron star. There's no way of telling."

"But supernovas and neutron stars occur all the time throughout the universe."

"In their own time. It's not the way of things for this to happen here, now, so quickly."

"And if you're left alone you'll simply add your mass to the nebula, gradually, the way it's been happening for eons."

She nodded.

"And that would eventually create another star."

Again, she nodded.

He managed a smile, stood. "Then I'll just have to come up with a plan." He turned away. "Won't I?"

What he didn't tell her was that he already had a plan. All he needed to do now was to gain the support of the hostages. Somehow, he knew he was spinning in the direction she chose to weave this tale.

There was a plan. Tine spoke of it eloquently enough to convince the hostages that it would work, that they needed to make it work. His threats to lay charges against those who had been involved with the Guild were probably the most convincing factors. None of them doubted he would do it. When faced with a Caliban in the hunter-mode, any argument would be convincing. The smile on Ela's face made him wonder if she hadn't been up to a little yarn spinning herself. If she had he was grateful. Somehow, he felt responsible for the plight of the dreamweavers.

Together, all thirty-three of them, trekked through the dreamlike regions of the southern latitudes. This would be their last night on the Skeins. Tomorrow they would reach Maxta and an end to the work-warrens. Tine had vetoed an assault on all the centres. That would only break their numbers. And it would also give undue opportunity to anyone still considering an alliance with the Guild.

At the moment, Tine's attention was within the fire Ela had woven, his senses following that vaporous woman. She grew paler with each day, less substantial. He wondered if she'd make it through this task.

The Gelt Ambassador diverted Tine's attention when he sank to the granite beside him.

"I hope she doesn't carry on the way she did last night."

Tine winced. Last night had been a gift to him, a tapestry of his brood, Aganth, a celebration of welcome, the ritual of acceptance. It was a gift he would cherish forever because Ela had woven a reality he hoped might exist.

"Is it so hard for you to understand that she has to weave at night?" he said at length.

"I think that's just an excuse."

Tine kept his gaze away from the Gelt. "Why would she lie?"

"To terrorize us."

"Why terrorize us? More your style."

"You really are a back-planet bumpkin."

Tine growled. Let the fool be afraid. Tine would have liked nothing better than to rip the Gelt's throat out, be done with his bias, and his avarice, and his need to control. He stared at the Gelt until he realized Tine expected an explanation, which came after a cluck of disgust.

"Isn't it obvious she's terrorizing us? The characters she incarnates are all from our memories."

"You think this is all some elaborate ruse?"

"Why not? If the dreamweavers really are an alien form, with all the power she demonstrates, they'd be capable of making us think anything."

"Or nothing. Hasn't it occurred to you they're crippled by their own capabilities? The children in the work-warrens are evidence enough."

     CALIBAN

"I've seen nothing of these work-warrens."

"Don't lie to me. Ela's told me of your eagerness to ally with the Guild in their takeover of the UOoP Chamber."

"I tell you I've seen no evidence of work-warrens."

"I have. They're real enough."

"What if they, also, are a tapestry? Have you thought of that?"

"Dreamweavers are capable of masking facts like the geography of the planet, but they are completely incapable of helping themselves to the extent you think."

The Gelt glared at him. "I think you're blind."

"I think you're too caught up in intrigue."

"What would you know of the workings of the real world?"

Tine seized the front of the Gelt's once-elaborate overcoat. The hell with diplomacy. "Setebos is as real as it gets," he snarled. "What would you know about a life free of avarice?" Tine shoved him away, surged upright and stalked off, letting the sound of his hooves punctuate his anger. None of the others came near him. Only their glances touched him—fearful, suspicious, edged with something that left bile on his tongue.

By the time Ela's weaving was full-blown, four moons had risen, arrayed like slices of melon across the sky. Tine watched from the perimeter of camp, listening to the mewling of a few of the hostages who were most affected by the tapestry tonight. Children watched from a distance, like scurrying rodents, their eyes bright, intent. For hours, they'd dogged

Tine's crew. He'd done everything to dissuade the wandering children of the Skeins from following. But they remained, now thrall to the tapestry Ela wove. There were threads around him also. He paid them little attention. Ela had taught him that. Reality was what you made it.

His gaze shifted to movement. Jabod. The Commissioner fidgeted, glancing periodically to where Tine squatted until finally he joined the Caliban.

"This doesn't bother you?" Jabod asked.

"What?"

"Her weaving?"

"Should it?"

"It bothers me."

Tine grinned. "Maybe living on an isolated planet has its advantages."

Jabod nodded to the others in camp. "How do you think they're going to face tomorrow?"

"Not very well."

"That's not too hopeful."

"It's realistic. Very few of them can accept what the dreamweavers do out here in the Skeins. You need to have a firm grip on your own reality to survive." He remembered Ela's words that first evening in the Skeins. She had given him a similar warning.

"And you don't think they do." Jabod said.

"No."

It sounded like an utter condemnation, as if he had decreed the doom of this plan, these hostages and the children in the other centres.

"We'll have no way of knowing till we get there," Jabod said.

That would be the worst of it. Just how prepared the Guild was for this eventuality not even Ela could say. Would they watch for her return? Would they suspect what she planned? There was little hope any of it would fall in their favour.

"Tell me, Jabod, how do you suppose this all got started?"

"All of what?"

"All of this—the slavery of the children. The complete lack of any evidence of a native alien race here."

Jabod's face was tight with frustration. "I don't know."

"Doesn't IPCIB have any kind of monitoring going on down here?"

"Limited. Only mechanical. The crimeless society here determined that."

"And all the time the most heinous crime of all was going on."

"There were no reports."

"Why should there be?"

"Are you accusing me?"

"Of ignorance. I'm accusing the Edain Guild of slavery. And I'm accusing people you thought were loyal of sabotage."

"Sabotage?"

"Hasn't it occurred to you that Luther is the key to all of this?"

"But—"

"He convinced you that I'd suffer from spore-withdrawal. The way I figure it, all of that was carefully prepared fifteen years ago, when the first group of Calibans tried to leave for Edain. My proof is that I've supposedly suffered spore-withdrawal, and yet the spore's still active."

"But—"

"Luther was the only one besides you who knew I was coming in to Edain as the Setebian Ambassador."

"That's all he knew. I didn't tell him you were going in as my Active."

"He still put it together."

Jabod paled. "Then wouldn't it be better for me to go back to the ship, prepare the proper charges and file them?"

"There isn't time. You know that. I've already told you that every time one of those children dies, a mature dreamweaver absorbs that mass. It's a critical situation here. We can't wait for lengthy court decisions." He looked directly at Jabod. "I'll be okay."

That was something Tine himself didn't believe. The Guild had managed to keep a rebellion from the IPCIB Commissioner. He wondered what else had been kept from Jabod. How long had this been going on? How extensive was the Guild's influence?

There was no point in continuing this discussion. Jabod had already taken enough blows for one evening, and Tine was loathe to hurt his friend. He still considered him a friend, even though at one point he'd entertained the thought of killing him.

Jabod paled. "I swear to you I knew nothing of any of this."

Another lie? Or just a need to redeem himself in Tine's opinion? Tine turned his back and pressed his side to the stone, letting his action give Jabod his answer, letting sleep take him away to a place Ela would understand.

Late the following day they all stood at the edge of the dome of Maxta where ersatz trees formed the perimeter parkland of the city, staring at the transparent material that separated them from their destination. It seemed so odd to Tine, less than a width of his hand beyond this was a controlled world of constant daylight, a world where everything made naturally was twisted into something called art. Suddenly paradise seemed more like Setebos than Edain. Beauty was how you perceived it.

Tine's attention shifted to the rear where the soft patter of feet gathered. A few of the borderland children crept through the crowd, wide-eyed, silent, as if they absorbed everything these adults did. Ela had tried to shoo them away but they clung to her like moths.

"I don't think this will work," Jabod said at length.

"We have to make it work," Tine answered, his gaze still piercing the dome.

"Us against all that?"

"We have to make it work."

"The odds are against us. Even if we were to get into into the city, do you really think the Guild won't have some kind of security network set up?"

Tine's attention swung to Jabod. He was aware his claws kept unsheathing. "You voted for this."

"It's a noble cause. But now, standing here, I know

we'll be defeated. This is the city where the Guild convenes, the centre of Edain."

"It is not the centre of Edain," Ela said.

"What? You think that place out there, out among your vaporous friends—that's the centre of Edain? We're not talking about principles here."

"Aren't we?" Tine said. "Isn't that why you voted for this plan? For the principle of it?"

"Well, yes, but—"

"Then we'll make it work." He didn't wait for Jabod to make any further protests. His attention shifted to Ela. "Will it be much longer?"

She shook her head. "The patrol for children should begin soon."

Tine shuddered. Such an abomination. When Ela first told him about the way the Guild went about finding candidates for dreamweaver apprentices he went numb with outrage. The Guild were so sure they were giving these children an advantage. It never occurred to them there was anything outside of their righteous mission.

It wasn't long before the patrol melted through the dome, spilling out to the borderlands like wooden soldiers. The weaving wasn't adept. But it was adequate.

Ela's eyes were wide with alarm. For a moment, Tine thought she was caught in memory, back to the time she'd been taken into the work-warrens. It was Jabod's reaction that gave him an answer to her emotion.

"IPCIB!" she said.

Jabod's face lit with relief.

IPCIB? Tine's gaze flicked around the patrol, catching a few Actives hidden in that mass, clear to anyone who knew what to look for, over to the Gelt who grinned that wolfish grin. Oil slicked Tine's skin. Alarm shouted through him, threatening to lead him on a rampage. But he held.

Why had Jabod been so happy to see his own Actives?

"I didn't tell the thread of you to authorize a landing party," Ela said.

"But obviously the captain of the ship did," Tine added.

Jabod's elation died. Tine need no prompting. There was nowhere to run. He'd stand and fight. It was plain these Actives had been sent in by the captain, the captain who was plainly in the pay of the Guild. Someone else was pulling authority in the Bureau.

Tine immobilized two of them before his opportunity to fight was denied. The troops were armed with stun-guns. Within moments the band of people were all down, dazed, even the children. The threads of the patrol dissolved, not in the way dreamweaver threads dissolved.

Hologram?

Tine looked around. It occurred to him the stun had little effect on him, perhaps because of his alien physiology. There was no sign of an imager for the holos. But the images had definitely not been of dreamweaver making. He knew that well enough by now.

The Active in charge of the troops strode over to Jabod, grinning. "We're going for a little ride,

Commissioner." He nodded to Tine and Ela. "The wart and the rebel are coming with us."

"The children," Jabod groaned.

The Active laughed. "They'll go where they belong—to the work-warrens."

Even now it was too late. The children were herded and jostled through an opening in the dome.

Tine tensed, ready to launch after the children. His attention shifted to Ela. Her body was a whisper of light, soft, subtle, plainly unaffected by the stun-guns. What was she doing?

A double of her now sat beside her, another, then another, until there were a dozen Elas all arrayed across the stone. A few rolled, stood, jostled with the others. All the time the troops tried to keep the real Ela in their sights, to no avail.

There was a shout of warning in Tine's mouth. What would happen if they shot her, this time with the real thing? Would she die? Would she remain unaffected? Or would that disaster she'd been avoiding occur?

"Let her go!" the officer growled, yanking Jabod to his feet. The Commissioner did nothing to help himself, his head lolling on his shoulders. The effect of the stun-gun was more than he could overcome.

Tine debated whether to maintain his ruse or fight. He glanced at the guns, the number of Actives. Perhaps it would be better to maintain his ruse. He could run, stand a chance of escaping before they shot him. But he'd still be as useless as if he'd been stunned. There would be no way he could get into and out of the work-warrens for the children without detection. He'd be as obvious as a blackout in Maxta.

Such an idea! A blackout! A blackout would work perfectly! Why hadn't he thought of that before?

Just as an Active was about to lay hands on him, he ducked away, tucked his legs under himself and set off in a sprint his pursuers would never be able to match. Disruption-shot striped the air around him. One hit. Heat seared his head. He growled. But he didn't stop running, now into the maze of Ela's clones, dodging, ducking, until one reached out her arms and wrenched him to a halt.

Tine's gaze zoomed to where the troops were taking aim. Light bloomed from the guns, extended, grew like a hot snake. So slow it seemed. All while Ela called out, "Wart! I need you!"

The cylinders of light were within hairs of the rug when he popped into the place of nothingness. If he could have found her, he'd have hugged Ela for joy.

*To this day I find it an irony that a hunter should
have placed his life in the hands of a dreamer.*

TINE

TIME STRETCHED. He was aware they were in the
between place. But it was taking so long. Or he
thought it was. Instinct told him to run, to hurl
himself from the rug—if he could feel where it was—
and take himself as quickly as possible to a place of
safety.

But that's what Ela was doing, wasn't she? How
could he tell? What was taking so long?

There was no wind pressing against his face.
Without that sensation, how could he tell if they
were moving? How did he know he wasn't just here,
in this nowhere? Maybe forever. He glanced around,
or thought he did. There wasn't even any light. But it
wasn't exactly dark, either. He blinked just to be sure
his eyes were open. The other times he'd travelled
this way there hadn't been anything to see. That
hadn't been a problem because it all happened so
fast. But now?

It's worse, he thought. *Why is Ela keeping us here?*
Which brought him to: what had gone wrong that Ela
needed to keep them so long in suspension?

He rubbed his eyes. Everything was dark,

impenetrable. Did that mean they'd arrived somewhere?

He looked up sharply, or at least what he thought was up. Here the darkness was peppered with golden lights, lights like those he'd seen from the children in the work-warrens. Beside him Ela also shone, sitting on her knees, her gaze beyond the Wart on the rug. It was plain she was weaving. He felt a kick of fear.

"What are you doing?"

What would happen if she wove with all these children? Would they be safe? Would she be safe?

"Something I should have thought of a long time ago."

"Tell me."

Her face turned toward him, her gaze touching him. "I'm becoming part of their reality."

"A part of.... What good will that do?"

"We'll shut down Maxta."

"You can do that? You can shut them down?"

"Everything's controlled here in the work-warrens—the light, the heat, everything."

So she'd thought of that too. Her way would be far more effective.

"Will it be safe?"

She turned her face back to the children. "Who knows?"

"You don't know?"

She shook her head. "Adult dreamweavers never weave with other dreamweavers. It's never been done before."

"Isn't there a possibility you could all—"

"Yes. That's why I'm going to get you out of here."

"No!" He grabbed her arm. "I won't let you!"

"You can't stop me."

"I won't leave you!"

"You have to, Tine. If this doesn't work, all these children will become part of me. That combined with the effect of the nebula and I'll have enough mass to create a star. Who knows what could happen? The only thing I'm sure of is that one way or the other I have to stop what's going on. There's at least hope in that."

"But if you fail, there won't be any more dreamweavers."

"There won't be any more dreamweavers here if I don't do this."

"But the risk! You could wipe out your whole race."

"Don't forget the dreamweavers on other planets in the UOoP. They'll be your responsibility if I fail." Her tone softened. "Please, Tine. This is the only way. IPCIB's in here with their troops. There's not much chance the Guild's going to make this any easier for us."

Deferring to her wasn't easy to swallow. But he accepted it. He knew her plan would be more than effective if it worked.

"What do you want me to do?"

"I'm going to send you to the liner with Wart."

"All that distance?"

"I have created and controlled threads in your solar system."

That she had. The representatives among her

hostages had come from every planet and satellite in the UOoP, and she'd controlled threads of them over all that distance. He'd have no need to worry about her ability.

"It's not very likely I'm going to be welcomed when I'm on the liner," he said.

"Welcomed or not, you're going to have to convince the captain that she must leave because of what could happen with me."

"That doesn't sound too promising."

She reached to pat his hand. Her fingers melted right through his flesh, withdrew. Tine longed to give her some word of consolation, but he could think of nothing. She smiled.

"It will be fine, Tine." She slid off the rug. "It's night again on Edain."

Tine contained his shock well. Now he had an answer to why they had been so long in that place between when Ela transported them. She had held them there, the only safe place, until night surrounded the city of Maxta. At night her weaving would be at its peak.

"Then you'll have time before the dawn," he said.

"To make fantasy reality."

For the first time in a long time Tine smiled.

He leaned forward on the rug and pecked her cheek, careful not to sink through her substance. In the next moment he was in that place between places, shivering, wondering if he'd ever see her again.

A perfect society would be a society of one. There can be no oppression, usury, misunderstanding or war with a society of one.

IPCIB Operations Manual.

"**Let her** go?" Tylan's leaves twitched. "What do you mean you let her go?"

The IPCIB Active glared at Tylan, wondering why she took this kind of abuse from a plant, intelligent though it might be.

"I let the dreamweaver go—yes," she answered. Her gaze shifted to the other three members of the Guild who were here, the Gelt, Luther from IPCIB. So much fuss over one dreamweaver.

"Do you have any idea what you let go?" Luther said. His anger seemed so out of place amid the forest.

"A dreamweaver. When it comes right down to it that's all she is. A dreamweaver."

"That *all* is more than you'll ever comprehend," Athran, the Master Painter, said.

"That was Master Ela you let go," the Gelt added.

Tylan twitched again. "She's the one who's orchestrated all of our plans."

"And now she's who knows where," Athran said.

"I'd like to see you catch her," The Active snapped.

"How hard could it have been?"

"There were at least a dozen clones of her. How was I to tell which was which?"

"By catching them all."

"All? With the limited crew Luther kept me to? Don't be ridiculous. What was I supposed to do—abandon the children, the hostages? Chase after her and that thing?"

"It would have been an improvement over this."

"Agreed," Hogan said, his twin concurring with him.

The Active snorted. "What the hell would you know about dealing with realities?"

"Have you any idea how real this situation's become?" Luther asked.

"No. But I'm sure you'll tell me."

"Your captain's just informed me that messages from all over the UOoP are coming in. It seems some very important dignitaries are disappearing—dissolving."

"That can only mean one thing," Tylan said.

"That Ela's let go of all the threads she wove for us," Athran said.

"Exactly."

"The UOoP Chamber's going to want some answers."

"There's nothing that can implicate us," Jen said.

"There's everything to implicate us," Tylan answered. "It's only a matter of time before someone figures out that the bodies of their VIPs dissolved in the way of a dreamweaver's thread. I can't think of any planet outside of Setebos that isn't well-acquainted with a dreamweaver's skills."

"So, that means we've got to find her," Luther said.

"And the Caliban?"

"I couldn't care less about the Caliban."

For just a moment the ever-present daylight flickered. Glances fired around the room.

"A hiccough," Hogan said.

The Active thrust her hands to her hips. "Just where do you expect me to start looking for this dreamweaver?"

Another flicker ran through Tylan's forest. Several trees dissolved.

"Having trouble with your systems?" Luther asked.

A look passed between Jen and Hogan.

"It would seem so," Athran answered.

"I still need to know where to start looking for her," the Active snapped.

A silent tremor ran through the forest, setting the trees into a chatter, the creatures into a cacophony.

"What was that?" Tylan screeched, his leaves swaying as if he were searching for a kill.

"I don't give a damn what that was," the Active yelled. "I have a job to do. Where do I start looking for Master Ela?"

Another tree dissolved, a fern, a hunk of ground.

"In the work-warrens," Tylan shrieked.

The next moment was one of blackness. Utter and complete. And then the sounds of screaming as buildings, homes, auto-systems failed all around them.

We're still searching. There's still so much we don't know about dreamweavers, but at least we do know what happens when they're put under pressure. It's a lesson none of us will soon forget.
REPORT FROM THE COMMISSION ON DREAMWEAVERS

THERE WAS nothing subtle about his entrance. Tine just popped onto the bridge of the IPCIB liner. His teeth chattered so loudly he could hardly hear, although what he did hear was the captain yelling, "Shit!"

That invective exploded again when the rug disappeared from under him and he fell into the captain's lap. When the invectives cleared and all that was left was the siren of a ship alert, Tine finally managed to untangle himself and stand, spouting apologies he hoped would mollify the captain.

Why had Ela disengaged the rug-rider so abruptly? Urgency needled him. He feared only the worst.

"Look what we've got here," the captain said. "A gargoyle."

Some of the crew laughed.

Tine let the insult slide. "You have to listen to me."

"I want to know how you breached my bridge."

"Later. There's a matter of—"

"I still want to know how you breached my bridge."

Tine heard her authority. There was no threat. Not yet. He kept his attention fixed on her.

"That's not important right now," he said. "You've got to evacuate Edain and get this ship out of here."

"Is that all?"

"I'm very serious."

"Give me a good reason why I should consider this."

"There's a possibility—just a possibility—that a star's going to detonate into existence out there."

"You're going to have to come up with something better than that."

"I'm telling you the truth. Edain's atmosphere is rich in hydrogen and helium because of the dreamweavers. You know what happens when enough of the stuff coalesces under pressure of gravity."

Her gaze never left him, although her voice reached for her science officer. "Check it out." Then to security. "Lock him up." She swivelled in her chair. "Get me a link with Luther."

Tine did nothing to resist when two security officers clamped his arms. Where could he run on a spacecraft?

When he was sealed into a guarded cell he sank to his haunches, munching a meal he'd called up from the self-serve. He just kept stuffing food between his canines, watching through the security field, listening. Would the captain find enough evidence to take his advice? Would Ela ever have the opportunity to evolve normally? Were the children free?

He hunkered on his haunches when done, waiting, hoping. Hours went by and still nothing seemed to be happening. Surely the captain wouldn't leave his

CALIBAN

suggestion untested? He opened his mouth to shout out, to make demands, but it wasn't like he had any room to bargain. What was needed was a strategy. He rose, paced his cell, always watching the three guards beyond. What else could he do? To rant and rave would serve no purpose. Anything might be happening to Ela and the children.

Pacing became wearisome. He lay upon the cot, rubbing oil into his hide, thinking of another cot, another cell, the deception, the elaborateness of the deception just to convince him he was free of the spore. In hindsight he realized how little they knew about living with the spore. It had only been a matter of time before Tine realized nothing had changed. All of this—his dealing with IPCIB, the Edain Guild, Ela—all had been falsehood upon falsehood coupled with illusions and vagaries.

When at last he fell asleep he thought he dreamed of illusions.

A dream. Ela. So real. Radiant as she sat at the foot of his cot, smiling that far-away smile for which he'd come to know her. Her arms were upon her thighs, her hands cupped as though revealing a treasure to him. In her palms clouds congealed, compressed, incandesced until he felt his whole world consumed in the magnitude of that shining blue ball that grew and grew so rapidly it was more an explosion. Its diamond brightness shifted to red. Even as that happened he was somehow able to see hydrogen bonding to hydrogen, creating helium, more bonding—oh no!— now carbon, now oxygen, neon, each element heavier than the next—oh no!—silicon, sulphur, a new core every time—oh no! oh no!—argon, calcium—oh sweet Ela, no! No! No!

Iron.

No more energy.

Contraction. Cataclysmic. His throat was tight with cries, his lips forming warnings no one heard. New elements in that contraction—gold, lead, uranium. So visible!

Collapse.

Just as if the shining ball had been fruit—squashed, layer upon layer falling inward. This couldn't go on forever. The core would stand only so much.

And then Tine felt the burst of tiny specks as they raced through him, feather-light, unbright, careening through the spaces and places of the universe no matter could go. He felt ghostly. Without substance. Dark matter incised him.

Dark matter!

Back, back, back across space, from where they raced—there, a hole, an abyss, a gate. A black star to steal light.

Ela!

He found himself awake, staring into the darkness of his cell, fear in his nose, his skin slick with oil.

Was it a dream?

Or had Ela come to warn him?

None of it had answer. Now belts from the cot claimed him, wrestling him down. Somewhere in the heart of the ship he could hear the distant whine of engines under stress, slammed into a leap through space. Wormhole! They were making a jump!

THE DREAM haunted Tine through the next hours. It coupled with his discomfort. Still the captain kept him bound to the bed, a captive now they'd completed the jump through space. It occurred to him his life might be worthless. Why would they need a him? Especially when he knew things he shouldn't—dangerous things, things that might unhinge the UOoP.

The sound of footsteps hauled him out of thoughts. His gaze darted to where the veil of light imprisoned him. The footsteps came from the other side of that curtain. The light paled, vanished. The captain stepped into his cell.

Tine's gaze swept over her. No weapons, at least none visible. This might not mean his death. That possibility did nothing to mitigate caution when the bonds around him retracted, or when the captain eased to the edge of his cot, her face unreadable.

"We've made a jump," he said after a moment. He weighed just what she might want with him.

She nodded.

"Then we're heading back to our home-system."

Again, she nodded.

"What now?"

"Now, in the immediate sense, I'll give you freedom to walk my ship. You're to talk to no one." She smiled, cold, calculated. "I wouldn't even bother to try if I were you. My crew have been instructed to ignore any of your comments."

"That's very thorough of you."

Again that cold smile.

"Are you afraid I'll spread heresy?"

The cold smile stiffened. "Don't push me."

"Then you mean to keep me alive."

"To dispose of you would raise too many questions."

"And what about when I'm back home?"

"IPCIB and the UOoP will destroy any record of you leaving Setebos, and of your involvement with the Bureau. That should discredit any charge you might want to file."

"That's convenient. And what about Setebos?"

"Still under quarantine."

"Again, convenient."

"Insurance."

"In case I decide to start mouthing some bizarre tale about the Edain Guild's support of slave trade, about the Guild's alliance with a treasonous faction in the UOoP planning to infiltrate and control the governments in the United Order of Planets, about corruption within IPCIB, about the suppression of information about a native, intelligent race on Edain."

"Just in case."

"What makes you think this will work?"

"Because no one wants to listen to a holy cause anymore. The people just want to be entertained. They want the Guild to survive, at any cost. How do you think the Guild managed to obtain a whole planet?"

"So why not just kill me?"

"That, also, would raise too much suspicion. Your kin would have to be notified of your whereabouts. How would we explain that you'd gone missing, or worse, that you'd died."

"I'm sure you'd find a way. It's not such a stretch given what you've done."

"This way's cleaner."

"And what about the Commissioner? What are you going to do about him?"

"He's already been dealt with."

Dealt with? Did that mean death? Had Jabod been sacrificed for their cause?

"How are you going to explain his death?"

"There's been an unfortunate accident in the city of Maxta. It seems the auto-systems failed, and the Commissioner plummeted to his death along with the Gelt Ambassador, Master Sculptor, Master Photographer and Master Holographer. We've had to send in IPCIB troops to deal with the rebels there. Any and all are to be annihilated." She rose. "You have two days before we arrive at Setebos. Enjoy your liberty."

When she left, the security systems remained inactive.

Tine didn't know how to feel. He was elated Ela managed to bring Maxta's systems to a halt. But he was also frantic to stop IPCIB's troops massacring the dreamweavers. A massacre could only lead to that end Ela predicted. But what could he do?

He was to return home, defeated, humiliated, without any evidence of the crimes of the Guild. Who would believe a backward Caliban? Especially a Caliban who claimed to have knowledge of a place he hadn't officially visited?

He swung his legs over the edge of the cot. He stood and walked out the door, down the corridor and wandered through thoughts and corridors. The people he passed stared through him as if he weren't there. Once, out of frustration, he stopped to ask for direction. The result was what he expected; no acknowledgement whatever. He would be a pariah, invisible for the next few days, perhaps the rest of his life. Who could tell what awaited him on Setcbos?

Anger threatened to consume him until he stared at a ship-directory and discovered there was an arboretum. His anger cooled, his path shifting.

Humidity clung to his hide when he stepped into the space-floating forest, the air vibrating to birdsong. He walked, touching the trunks, allowing the forest to fill him.

There had been another forest, gnarled trees, leaves of red, yellow, purple, harps moaning against the touch of the wind. For a moment memory of it transformed this forest. Only for a moment. When he came to the edge of the dome, where the forest gave way to the spectacle of space, he growled, baring his teeth against the futility of it all.

Stars bled by like ribbons of rainbows. He wondered if any one of these might be Ela's parents, her brothers, her sisters. Would he look up to the sky one night and find her there?

At that moment one of the ribbons burst into brilliance. He ducked his head into his hands, crying out against pain. Another part of him screamed out to see what had happened, his fingers splaying, shielding his eyes. Everything was dominated by a tube of whiteness, a tube that swirled like a corona around a place of utter blackness, a place where light couldn't penetrate.

The Edain nebula was gone.

He mouthed two syllables. He fell to his haunches, head in hands, and wept Ela's name, wept it like an anthem that would give him courage to wage an unlikely battle.

The original idea that dreamweavers were incompatible with other intelligent life, we believe, is now unfounded. We're living with them on Setebos without difficulty. Perhaps we should rephrase that statement of incompatibility to say that dreamweavers are unable to live with intelligent life that deviates from the animal state. Sometimes more doesn't necessarily mean better.

REPORT FROM THE COMMISSION ON DREAMWEAVERS.

THE YELLOW jasmine was in bloom. It cloaked this hemisphere of Setebos with golden flowers and rich fragrance, something that happened in the season of Seihung. In the midst of a meadow of the delicate shrubs, Aganth stood. Tine had his back to her, staring at their hut. It still reminded him of the carcass of a worm, the way it hugged the land, irregular, winding, without any of the structure or rhythms of civilization. This was something he thought he'd never see again. Seeing it now....

He swallowed emotion, hot and immediate: grief, joy, hope, despair. He never thought he'd feel this again, not after knowing what happened to Ela, not after his journey back to his home.

He turned to where Aganth stood, took in her brown, leathery face, the warts almost purple, flushed with health. By everything he held sacred she was beautiful to him.

"I was wrong," he said, letting the simplicity of his words lay before her. An offering. He'd approached her with caution, careful to do nothing to alarm her, careful to keep everything about himself submissive.

She remained perched on the edge of a rock, her legs dangling into the fragrant jasmine. Sunset gilded her face. She made no response.

"You were right," he continued. "I can't run from what I am. I don't think I want to." He gestured to the landscape, their hut. "This is what I am. I'm Setebos." He lowered his arm, muscles cording like serpents. "If you'll have me. I'd like you to have me."

Still Aganth made no response. She hummed, a sound like bees stirring through the jasmine. It was more than Tine could hope. This song was more than he deserved.

The children of his brood popped out of nowhere, some from the perfume-covered ground, some leaping from the overhang behind Aganth, others racing from the hut. They ringed him round with sound, moving to a rhythm which at first seemed irregular, later would become intricate, without regard for time, a ring of movement that orbited his nexus, touched and spun away. It was the ritual of welcome. It was the ritual of return. It was the ritual that would again integrate him into the way of Caliban life.

So it was that he found his vows renewed, his place within his family restored.

When the youngest of his brood scampered away, singing a song to praise his father, Aganth let her fingers touch the warts on Tine's face. He longed to spill out his words to her, to let them heal all that burned, to allow a bond of peace between them. Tears held them all. Tears did what words could not.

Aganth clucked her tongue, smiling, her canines bright now that night had taken the land.

"I am with child, Tine."

Laughter filled his mouth. That, apparently, was all the reply she needed. She turned him toward their bower where they would greet the rising moons with their caresses.

Later that night, when Aganth had sung the evening song and his family slept, he sat outside. There was a hole in the sky where the Edain nebula should have been. He wondered what Ela thought of her new existence, how the children she had taken with her fared. What was it like to live in legion?

He sketched a screen in the air, watched it materialize. The first thing he would do would be to make contact with the dreamweavers on the other planets in the UOoP. They'd be sure to help him lay charges once he offered them passage to Setebos. His wealth would serve a purpose now. He'd purchase them a safe place aboard insignificant freighters, shipping them all out of reach of the UOoP's traitors. With the evidence these dreamweavers could give, they who had worked so closely with Ela, the Guild's guilt would be revealed. And that might help to prevent another Edain from occurring.

The easiest thing he ever did was to establish a link to the Gelt Consortium's dreamweaver. All he said was, "I know."

The dreamweaver's response was: "We're waiting.

About the Author

Lorina Stephens is an editor, freelance journalist for national and regional print media, author of six books both fiction and non-fiction, a festival organizer, publicist, lectures on many topics from historical textiles and domestic technologies, to publishing and writing; teaches, and continues to work as a writer, artist, and publisher.

She has had several short fiction pieces published in *On Spec*, *Postscripts to Darkness*, *Neo-Opsis*, *Deluge*, *Strangers Among Us,* and *Sword & Sorceress X.*

Lorina Stephens is presently working on a new novel entitled, *The Rose Guardian,* and another, *Brogan's Folly.*

She lives with her husband of four plus decades, in a historic stone house in Neustadt, Ontario.

Books by Five Rivers

NON-FICTION

Big Buttes Book: Annotated Dyets Dry Dinner, (1599), by Henry Buttes, with Elizabethan Recipes, by Michelle Enzinas

Al Capone: Chicago's King of Crime, by Nate Hendley

Crystal Death: North America's Most Dangerous Drug, by Nate Hendley

Dutch Schultz: Brazen Beer Baron of New York, by Nate Hendley

Forgotten Injustice: The Ron Moffat Story, by Nate Hendley

John Lennon: Music, Myth and Madness, by Nate Hendley

Motivate to Create: a guide for writers, by Nate Hendley

Steven Truscott, Decades of Injustice by Nate Hendley

King Kwong: Larry Kwong, the China Clipper Who Broke the NHL Colour Barrier, by Paula Johanson

Shakespeare for Slackers: by Aaron Kite, et al
  Romeo and Juliet
  Hamlet
  Macbeth

The Organic Home Gardener, by Patrick Lima and John Scanlan

Shakespeare for Readers' Theatre: Hamlet, Romeo & Juliet, Midsummer Night's Dream, by John Poulson

Shakespeare for Reader's Theatre, Book 2: Shakespeare's Greatest Villains, The Merry Wives of Windsor; Othello, the Moor of Venice; Richard III; King Lear, by John Poulsen

Beyond Media Literacy: New Paradigms in Media Education, by Colin Scheyen

Stonehouse Cooks, by Lorina Stephens

FICTION

Black Wine, by Candas Jane Dorsey

Eocene Station, by Dave Duncan

Immunity to Strange Tales, by Susan J. Forest

The Legend of Sarah, by Leslie Gadallah

The Empire of Kaz, by Leslie Gadallah
  Cat's Pawn
  Cat's Gambit

Growing Up Bronx, by H.A. Hargreaves

North by 2000+, a collection of short, speculative fiction, by H.A. Hargreaves

A Subtle Thing, by Alicia Hendley

The Tattooed Witch Trilogy, by Susan MacGregor
  The Tattooed Witch
  The Tattooed Seer
  The Tattooed Queen

A Time and a Place, by Joe Mahoney

The Rune Blades of Celi, by Ann Marston
  Kingmaker's Sword, Book 1
  Western King, Book 2
  Broken Blade, Book 3
  Cloudbearer's Shadow, Book 4
  King of Shadows, Book 5
  Sword and Shadow, Book 6
A Still and Bitter Grave, by Ann Marston
Indigo Time, by Sally McBride
Wasps at the Speed of Sound, by Derryl Murphy
A Quiet Place, by J.W. Schnarr
Things Falling Apart, by J.W. Schnarr
A Poisoned Prayer, by Michael Skeet
And the Angels Sang: a collection of short speculative fiction, by
  Lorina Stephens
Caliban, by Lorina Stephens
From Mountains of Ice, by Lorina Stephens
Memories, Mother and a Christmas Addiction, by Lorina Stephens
Shadow Song, by Lorina Stephens
The Mermaid's Tale, by D. G. Valdron

YA FICTION

Eye of Strife, by Dave Duncan
Ivor of Glenbroch, by Dave Duncan
  The Runner and the Wizard
  The Runner and the Saint
  The Runner and the Kelpie
Avians, by Timothy Gwyn
Type, by Alicia Hendley
Type 2, by Alicia Hendley
Tower in the Crooked Wood, by Paula Johanson
A Touch of Poison, by Aaron Kite
The Great Sky, by D.G. Laderoute
Out of Time, by D.G. Laderoute
Diamonds in Black Sand, by Ann Marston
Hawk, by Marie Powell

WWW.FIVERIVERSPUBLISHING.COM

Eocene Station
ISBN 9781988274058
eISBN 9781988274058
by Dave Duncan
Trade Paperback 6 x 9
October 1, 2016

A new Dave Duncan novel is always a reason to celebrate, and his trademark blend of high adventure, hard science, and wry humour makes *Eocene Station* a must read.

K. N. 'Cannon' Ball and his superstar wife, Tempest, are running for their lives. Cannon has exposed a fraud so huge even heads of government are implicated and determined to keep Cannon from ever testifying. Nowhere is safe, so they step out of time to a research station fifty million years in the past. The dinosaurs died out eons ago and there aren't any people around, so they ought to be safe then, right? Wrong, very wrong!

Absolutely smashing.
Goodreads

...brilliant settings, plot, action and character development...
entirely enjoyable.
LibraryThing

Shadow Song
ISBN 9780973927818
eISBN 9780986563041
by Lorina Stephens
Trade Paperback 6 x 9
September 1, 2008

Vengeance in the backwoods of Upper Canada. An uncle insane with retribution, a midewiwin following a vision, and the girl caught between both worlds.

Danielle Michele Fleming, 10 year old daughter of a French aristocratic mother, and the second son of English gentry, finds herself caught in the economic ruin that surrounds the failure of the Bourbon Monarchy. She finds herself aboard ship, destined for the Queen's Bush of Upper Canada and a life with the catalyst of her doom, her uncle, Edgar Fleming. Relentless in his hunt for her, her uncle has her tracked not only by bounty hunters, but in the end through another shaman of evil intent and a blood-debt to settle with Shadow Song.

Lorina Stephens has proven herself an engaging author.
The (Hanover) Post

The book Shadow Song is as diverse as the woman who wrote it.
Susan Doolan, The Barrie Examiner

From Mountains of Ice
ISBN 9780973927856
eISBN 9780986563027
by Lorina Stephens
Trade Paperback 6 x 9
September 1, 2009

Sylvio spent the past decade banished from Simare's court, stripped of land, ancestral home and title – from Minister of National Security to back-country bowyer. But not any bowyer; Sylvio creates bows from laminations of wood and human bone, bows that are said to speak, bows known as the legendary arcossi.

And now, after a decade, he is called back to the capitol, summoned by his Prince whom he suspects is a patricide and insane. His very life is in danger and with it the country he has served through all his days.

From Mountains of Ice is a story of love, endurance and the meaning of honour.

From Mountains of Ice is an entertaining and original fantasy from Lorina Stephens, highly recommended.

Midwest Book Review

...a non-stop ride filled with surprises at every turn.

The Little Red Reviewer